SOMEWHERE IN-BETWEEN
AN ADVENTURE IN THE AFTERLIFE

WENDY FEDAN

i

FOR MY DAD, BOB CARRICK.
(1945-2017)

CONTENTS

ACKNOWLEDGMENTS

Much appreciation to all my Beta Testers:

Abby & Katie Adams, Alex Allen, April Johnson, Tracy Kelly, Olivia Kmiec, Hannah Leduc, Cyndi Liming, Kym McBride, Rosemary Nagay, Pam Strohmeyer, Carol Ward.

Thank you all so much for your help reviewing this book!

SPECIAL THANKS

To Cyndi Liming for her generous support, encouragement and friendship on her "Bus of Awesomeness!"

To Joan Little for her help with the initial editing of this project.

To Kym McBride for her generous input and incite.

CHAPTER 1 - THE CHOICE

Green car. Sister screaming in the back seat. Loud crash. Shattering glass.

The accident happened when Max's mom was driving him home from picking up his kid sister, Perry, from daycare.

I guess I shouldn't have insisted on having the front seat, he thought as he saw the green car appear from nowhere and hit his side of the car straight-on. He remembered thinking it was exactly the car he was hoping to get when he was old enough to get his own license – but that wouldn't be for another couple years – he hoped.

It's amazing how quickly thoughts go through your head in a single second. The glass showering him had fragmented into tiny cubes. He squinted his eyes to protect them. He felt the force of the impact on his body, but where was the pain? It was strong, but only lasted for a millisecond.

And what was with this bright light surrounding him? Max thought. *Then again, where was the car?* He couldn't see anything but this weird light all around. He had lost all feeling, too. *Am I paralyzed? I was just in a car crash. I must have been knocked out.*

Then came the fear. Or was it more like panic? The feeling you get when you wake up the first day of vacation and you can't remember where you are. Yeah, that was it. But this feeling wasn't going away quickly enough. Instinctively, he tried calling out. "Hello! Hello, can anybody hear me?" His voice sounded strange. The same way he remembered sounding when he wore earplugs and tried to speak. So strange.

Max strained to hear an answer.

"Hello!" Max repeated. "Can anyone hear me?!"

Max was just about to start crying, when finally he heard a voice answer him. "Yes, Max, don't worry, I'm here."

It sounded like someone was standing right behind him, and he swung around to see who it was. Nobody was there. "Who are you? Where are you?" The fear was real, now. "What's going on?" His voice was shaking. "What's happening to me?"

The light around him suddenly felt thick, like it had substance to it. He felt it closing in on him, but it didn't scare him. It felt comforting, like a... like a warm hug. The tears finally came, and he began to sob, overcome with emotion. "What's happening to me? Please tell me. Please help me!"

"Be not afraid, Max." There was that warm hug again. "Come with me, and I will give you rest."

Those words struck him so powerfully. It was like an electric charge went through him, erasing his fear. For that moment he didn't care where he was or what was happening to him. He trusted this light and this voice. He felt like he was home. *Home... Home... Wait a minute...* "Wait!" Max stopped himself. "What about my mom and sister? Are they here too?" He looked around again. Nope still alone. Just him and this voice.

No answer. Silence.

"Where's my mom and sister?" He repeated. "Please! Tell me where they are?"

Finally an answer, but this voice was different, and it startled him. "They're not ready to come home yet, Max."

Max turned and saw a tall, slender woman. She looked old enough to be his grandmother, but she stood straight and tall. She had a magical quality, like she stepped out of a Lord of the Rings movie, but her hair was very short. Her hair and gown were the same color as the light that surrounded them, so she seemed to almost be a part of the light herself. Max was stunned, and stammered to find his words. "Are... are you?" He gulped. He was afraid to ask. "Are you my...?"

"Guardian angel?" The woman smiled. "Yes, I'm one of them. One of many."

Max was struck by the sudden realization. The shock was over. "Wait a minute, wait!" Max shook his head. "Am I dead, or something? Am I DEAD?"

"*You're* not dead, Max. Your *body* is dead. Your spirit is very much alive, but to stay that way, you need to come with me now, before the light fades."

"What happens when the light fades?" Max asked.

"The light is what carries you home. It comes for every spirit when the body dies. This is the moment for every man to make his final choice."

"What choice?"

"The choice to come home or to stay."

"Wow, I actually have a choice about that?"

The Angel nodded. "Time to come home now, Max. Come." She reached her hand out calmly, with a peaceful smile.

5

"Wait, though," Max thought. "You said I had a choice. What happens if I stay here? Will I get to go back to my mom and sister? I mean, what if they do CPR on me and bring me back to life? Do I still have a chance?"

The Angel's smile faded. "Your body is beyond repair, I'm afraid. And your sister's body will soon be the same."

"No!" Max gasped. "No! You mean little Perry's dying?"

The Angel looked at him inquisitively. "Why does this distress you, Max?"

His anger welled up. "Oh, 'How does this distress me?' Seriously? My baby sister is about to die, and you ask me why I'm distressed?"

Her face was unchanged. "Yes. Why, Max?"

"Well, DUH! I mean, HELLO! Because she's barely had a chance to LIVE! She's just a toddler! And I'm just a teenager! I mean, it's not fair! It's not fair!"

"Not fair? What's not fair about it, Max?" Her countenance grew serious. "You speak as if living in a body is the sole purpose of your existence."

"Huh? What are you talking about?"

"Max," she stepped close and took his hand in hers, "come home with me, and you will see clearly. There is far too much to explain. You only understand life on Earth, because it is all you know. That life is over now. A new life has begun... a new existence. I know this is hard for you, because you were just getting used to your life on Earth, in the body. But there is so much more you can accomplish in the spirit. You and your sister. It is time to come with me now, Max. The light can only last so long in this plane."

"What plane? An airplane? Final destination: Death Valley?"

She smiled, amused, and shook her head. "No, Max. I mean this plane of existence. The three-dimensional plane. Earth."

6

"Wait, we're still on Earth? I'm still on Earth! I'm still home! Can I please stay? I want to stay here with my family. I have to!"

This was the first time he saw a look of concern on the Angel's face. "No, Max."

"What do you mean, no? Didn't you tell me I had a choice? I want to stay and be here when Perry dies. Then we can go with you together!"

"Max, no."

"Why not?!"

"It is dangerous for you here, in the In-Between. Max, you must come with me, away from this place."

Max looked around him at the light. He noticed it was starting to fade, and he could vaguely see they were in the Rite Aid parking lot. It was right by the intersection of Leavitt Road and Cleveland Avenue, where the accident took place. Seeing familiar surroundings gave him comfort. "I have to stay," he said. "I have to stay and wait for Perry. Then I'll come with you, okay?"

The Angel looked at him with disappointed eyes, and stepped backward into the fading light. "Before I go, I must warn you, Max. Stay away from the darkness. The In-Between is not a place of safety. On earth there is danger of losing your life, but in this place there is danger of losing what is truly valuable... your soul." She was fading away with the light, and Max could barely hear her final words to him. "The light will appear again for your sister, Max. Be sure you are present when she is ready to come home. I hope you are able to join her."

The light was gone now. Max found himself alone in the Rite Aid parking lot, just outside downtown Amherst, Ohio. Everything looked so different. There wasn't a car in sight. It was like... *a ghost town.* Max chuckled nervously at that thought.

"Well," Max said to himself, "I sure hope I made the right choice."

CHAPTER 2 - GHOST TOWN

As Max walked down Cleveland Street, the term "Ghost Town" felt a little too close to home. It wasn't just the streets that were empty. The houses looked vacant as well. Where were the cars? There wasn't a single driveway with a car in it. Thank goodness home was close by. Someone had to be home, he thought. Mom and Dad would be there, and if they weren't, he would try the hospital next. Max halted at that thought. *Oh, no. Where is the hospital?* "Oh, man," he muttered. Never having driven himself anywhere, he had no clue. "This is going to suck big time."

His walk turned to a jog and then to a run. He needed to get home now. Needed to see home... be home. He realized quickly that running was easy. There was no running out of breath. He was running so fast, he felt like he was almost flying down the street - like he didn't even have to move his legs. He moved faster and faster. "Oh, man! Oh, man!" he stammered as he realized he had no idea how to slow himself down. *No body anymore! I have no weight. No weight, no gravity!* Max let out a yelp, pushing his arms forward. Every bit of energy inside him was saying, "STOP!" And quickly he came to a halt, like the jolting stop at the end of a roller coaster ride. "Whoa! Oh, jeez, man. This will be really hard to get used to."

Faintly, Max could hear laughter. Searching for the sound, he was thrilled when he saw an old man on a porch up ahead. The man was sitting relaxed, cross-legged on a porch swing. It was one of Amherst's grandest century homes on Cleveland Avenue, on the corner of the Maude Park entrance. Max walked or rode by it almost every day of his life, and he never saw anyone there before. "Hey!" Max called out and moved toward him - careful this time, not to get too carried away. He didn't want to accidentally end up nearly flying again. "Hey, you!"

"Hey yourself, kid!" The man said lightly. He didn't get up from his seat. He stayed in his position, legs crossed, arm out beside him. The classic pose of a man relaxed on a porch swing. "Looks like you're having some trouble adjusting." He chuckled, and shook his head with amusement. "Heh, Heh! I sure love watching the new folks arriving. It's the only entertainment you get around here."

Max knew the old man was picking fun at him, but he didn't care. He was overjoyed to see another person in what appeared to be an otherwise abandoned town. He decided to introduce himself. "My name's Max."

"Hi there, Max! I'm John." His pose didn't change, Max noticed. The man nodded toward the end of the street where the Rite Aid was. "I saw you in the light, over there. What made you decide to stick around here, kid? Ain't nothin' here but dead people, and they're no fun, lemme tell ya."

No small talk in the afterworld, Max noticed. "I stayed to wait for my sister. She's dying, and I'm guessing she must be in the hospital.

But, but..." Max looked around. "I have no idea how to get there."

John shook his head slowly, smiled, and chuckled again. "Oh, son, you've made one heck of a mistake."

Max's anger was returning. "Hey, what do *you* know about anything? You don't know me!"

"I know you're a moron, kid, that's what I know." The old man kept his relaxed demeanor and didn't budge.

Well this is just great, Max thought. The first person I meet in the afterlife and he's a cranky old geezer.

"I tell you what, kid. I'm gonna tell you everything you need to know." The laughter went out of the old man's face completely, and grew stone serious. "Stay away from the Living. You want to help your sister, your momma, your papa?" His body finally moved, but slowly. His relaxed demeanor changed completely. The old man sat straight with both legs planted firmly on the porch floor, his body leaning forward with purpose. "You leave them alone. You hear me, son? Leave...them... alone."

Max backed up and started back down the porch steps to the sidewalk. He didn't speak. Creepy old man, he thought. What does he know? He certainly wasn't going to help him find the hospital. "Good to meet you, John," Max said. "But I don't care what you say. I'm going to find my sister. She needs me."

John barked out a laugh so loud, it almost knocked Max over. "She needs YOU, eh? She needs you like a hole in the head, kid! You need HER! You need HER, boy!" His voice was angry.

Max started to run again. He wanted to get as far away from this old guy as he could. The farther he ran, the louder the old man called out to him.

"That life is over, and you gotta deal with it, boy! You hear me?! Let your people go! You're no good to them now!"

If Max had a body, he knew he would be feeling sick right now. Old man John had to be wrong. He had to just be a cranky, crazy old geezer. The fearful thought crossed his mind that maybe he did make a terrible mistake. He made it all the way to Five Points — the intersection of five streets in downtown Amherst. Still no cars. Nowhere. Nothing. And where were all the other dead people in the world? The old man said this place was "full of dead people." So where were they? Max stood alone in the middle of Five Points, a place when alive he would never be able to stand with all the traffic. He sat there, cross-legged, and cried. No tears, no mucous, but he wept the only way he could. The thought occurred that maybe he should try to pray, and he gave it a try. I mean, why not? He thought. I'm probably closer to wherever God is than I was when I was alive, right? Max folded his hands in his lap and gave it a whirl. "God please help me," he whimpered. "Can you please help me find my sister?" He remembered what the angel said to him before the light dissipated. She told him to be present when his sister's light arrived. Max gasped at this and shot up on his feet. "I can't miss the light again!" He said aloud to himself. "Oh my gosh, that old man John was right! I need Perry. I need to get back to the Light!" Max looked up. Up was where heaven was, right? "Please! Help me! Where is the hospital? Where is the hospital?!!" His voice grew desperate.

Suddenly he heard a noise he thought he would never hear again. The sound of a car engine. A silver Toyota Camry was waiting at one of the stop signs. Max squinted. He couldn't believe what he was seeing. There was a woman in the driver's seat, but she was almost transparent. In the back seat there was a girl, somewhat transparent, but a little more solid. And she had a glow around her. Max was confused. Was this another angel, come to answer his prayer... in a Toyota Camry? The girl was looking right at him. She stared, wide eyed, with a look of complete surprise. She seemed as surprised to see him as he was to see her.

And then he recognized her. It was Lizzie Boggs from his Language Arts class. "Dizzy Lizzie" everyone called her in class. She was always an odd girl, keeping to herself all the time, always reading those weird Manga books. The car sped up through the intersection, and Max ran over to it. He didn't care if it was weird Dizzy Lizzie. He just knew he needed to talk to her. She was glowing, just like the angel. Was she dead too? "Lizzie! Lizzie, it's me, Max Fletcher! Lizzie, can you hear me?!" As the car came closer he could see her tears. Lizzie closed here eyes tight and pressed her hands against her ears.

"Lizzie, no! Lizzie!" He called out, but the car kept driving away, and faded into nothingness the farther it drove down Cleveland Avenue.

CHAPTER 3 - LIZZIE BOGGS

"Lizzie, are you okay? Why are you crying?" Lizzie's mom asked, concerned. Lizzie had been crying a lot in the past couple years. She'd gone through therapy to help her, but there didn't seem to be much of a change.

"Sorry, mom," Lizzie wiped her face. "I was just thinking about a boy at school who died recently."

Her mother grew more concerned. "Oh, honey, I'm sorry. I didn't hear about that. Was he a friend of yours?"

Friend of mine? Lizzie almost laughed inside. She hated that Max kid. He was one of the boys that always teased her. But she couldn't tell her mom the truth about why she was crying, so she let it go. "I was just thinking about his family, that's all. They must be pretty sad about what happened. It's just a sad thing."

"Have you talked to Dr. Lewis about this at all?" Her mom asked, cautiously. They agreed way back that what was discussed in therapy stayed in therapy, but there were times her mom slipped up. She was just so worried about Lizzie. She never talked about friends, and when the family wanted to go out anywhere for fun, Lizzie seemed very withdrawn. She insisted on bringing her MP3 player everywhere, listening to her loud music all the time.

"Mom, remember, I don't want to talk about my therapy stuff." Lizzie crossed her arms.

Mrs. Boggs raised a hand. "Sorry, sorry. I know. End of subject, okay?"

They turned off Cleveland Street, onto Forest Road, and a quick left behind the graveyard. Lizzie wondered why the heck her parents decided to buy a house by the graveyard, and she wondered if that was the cause of the problems she'd been having.

After helping her mom bring the groceries inside, Lizzie went straight upstairs to her room. She always kept her blinds closed, because she was the lucky one with the graveyard view from her bedroom. *And they wonder why I need therapy*, she thought to herself.

She plopped onto the bed and reached for her headphones. She scanned through the selections on her MP3. What will it be today? She mused. Lindsey Stirling? Ane Brun? She decided on Peter Gabriel. Her dad got her into that artist, as he did with most of the music she decided she loved, and listening to it always made her feel good, thinking of him.

As the tunes soothed her, she also hoped it would tune out anyone who tried contacting her again. She placed crosses all around her room, hoping that would protect her against her daily intruders. One over her door, one over her window, and one over her bed, just for extra security.

She reached for the journal she kept on her nightstand, her Totoro pen, and began her afternoon routine. It was part of her therapy to keep a daily journal.

Today sucked, she wrote. *I wish I could just make them stop coming to me. I don't understand. What is it about me, anyway? Why doesn't anyone else see them the way I do?* Her tears started to come again. She angrily wiped them away. *Everyone thinks I'm crazy. Maybe I am. They come to me so often now, and I don't seem to be safe anywhere. They come to me at school, at the grocery store, at restaurants, even my own home. These dead people – they keep coming to me, asking for help. How on earth can I help them? What do they want from me? And how do they know to come to me anyway? I try ignoring them and they still come. Every day. EVERY DAY.*

    I even saw one from the car on my way home today. More tears came as she remembered. *It was terrible. I can still hear him calling out my name. It's the first dead person I've seen that I actually recognized, and he knows my name! His name is Max. I remember him from school. He and his friends always made fun of me. They called me "Dizzy Lizzie."*

    Lizzie paused, and frowned. *Max Fletcher has another thing coming if he thinks he's getting any help from me. What kind of help does he want from me anyway?* She remembered the desperate look on Max's face. He looked so afraid, so lonely. For a kid who never cared about her when he was alive, he sure seemed to want to talk to her now that he was dead. Why was that, anyway? Lizzie continued to write.

    It must be pretty lonely on the other side if someone like Max Fletcher suddenly becomes so desperate to talk to me. He looked at me as if he wanted me to save him from something. But save him from what?

    Her thoughts wandered as she continued to move the pen.

    I really don't understand why or how these dead people are even around. I believe in heaven and hell, but what is with these dead people? They seem to me like they're stuck in a place where they don't

belong. Could it be that there is a place that exists – kind of like
purgatory. A place... somewhere in between heaven and hell? She
paused again, wondering further, continuing to write as if in a trance.
The people who come to see me always seem to want my help. I keep
wondering what kind of help they're looking for. What is it that they
think I can do for them? What makes me so special?

Lizzie froze at that thought, and immediately scowled at
herself. With a snort, she scribbled out that sentence. "*What makes*
you so special, Lizzie Boggs? Nothing! Who do you think you are?!"
She sneered at herself.

She slammed the journal closed, tossed it back onto her
nightstand, and threw the pen across the room. The sobbing started
back up again as she lay on her back, hands pressed against her face,
listening to Peter Gabriel's "Don't Give Up."

CHAPTER 4 - THE MURAL

After Lizzie's car disappeared, Max stood in the center of Five Points, deciding it was time to just head home. He needed to get to the hospital, but without someone to help point the way, how would he even find it? Maybe mom and dad would be home, he hoped. He longed for a welcoming familiar face. He could feel fear and sadness taking over him and he needed to stop it.

Although Cleveland Avenue was normally his route to get home, he decided to take an alternate route. The last thing he needed was to run into that old cranky guy again. Max walked down Park Avenue, through downtown Amherst. It was so strange. Although Amherst was a small town, there was normally a lot going on in the little downtown area. There were restaurants and shops, business offices, a little barber shop, a coffee shop, bars, a tattoo parlor, yoga studio, and even a little movie theater that only showed one film at a time. Downtown Amherst was always busy, but now it looked emptier than a Sunday morning. As he approached the edge of downtown, something caught his eye in the parking lot, on the side of the last building. Normally on this wall would be the Veteran's Mural. This mural wall was the pride of Amherst, honoring the memories of local heroes. It was a four-part mural, remembering the wars of World War Two, Korea, Vietnam, and the Middle East. The faces of the departed were incorporated in that mural, and every Veteran's Day the town performed a ceremony in front of that mural to honor local veterans.

He looked at the wall now. The mural images were all gone, and replaced by one large mural. It was completely different. On the left, there was a painting of what looked like the sun. In the middle, there was the earth, half in light, half in shadow. The right side faded into blackness. As he looked closer, he could faintly see figures in the blackness. Some looked like people, wailing. And some figures in the darkness looked more like creatures. They looked like the kind of creatures you'd see in a horror movie, demon-like with vicious teeth and claws. Their bodies were dark, crooked and boney. These beings were holding the people down into the blackness as they reached hopelessly toward the earth and the light. Some, he could see, were coming out of the dark side and leaping toward the earth, claws extended, jaws open. Some had their claws into the earth, and some had people riding on their backs from earth, into the blackness. The image gave Max the creeps, and he had to look away.

He walked closer to the sunny end of the mural instead, turning his back to the other side. There, he could see people from earth riding the backs of what looked like angels as they flew from the earth into the light. The people in the light were not what he expected. He expected to see dancing, singing, rejoicing. Instead there was a giant hand in the center of the sun, pointing a commanding finger toward the earth. The figures coming out of the light looked much like the angel Max first met after the accident. There were so many of them, and they were moving toward earth with such determination, they resembled an army.

As he looked closer, he walked to the center of the mural, getting a final good look at the earth itself. The first half, toward the light, had illustrations of people doing normal things: walking dogs, carrying shopping bags, driving cars. The people painted on the bright side of earth seemed pretty oblivious to what else was going on in the mural. The people painted on the dark half of the earth, however, were all facing the bright side, arms outstretched, as if trying to take them over to he dark side with them. Some were reaching for the light side of the earth while one of the creatures from the blackness grabbed them by the feet. Max felt he understood what this mural was telling him. It was an illustration of heaven and hell, with earth in the middle. He imagined the bright side of earth must be the side with the living, and the dark side of earth must be where he was stuck right now. But there was one aspect of the mural he couldn't understand. On the dark side of earth, there was one small person painted with arms outstretched, painted in white and yellows. He couldn't see anything to help him understand the significance of who this person was supposed to be, but it was painted with the same colors as used in the heavenly side of the painting.

"Do you like it?"

Max was startled by the voice that called out behind him. He turned around, but there was nobody there.

"Up here!" He heard it again, and looked up. There, sitting on the top of the coffee shop was a woman dressed in what looked like colorful rags.

"Oh, hi!" Max was so startled, he didn't know what to say. Still unsettled by the last dead person he had a conversation with, he was tentative.

"You didn't answer me!" The woman called down. "Do you like my mural?"

"Oh," Max stammered. "Yeah. Yeah, it's nice."

"Well, that's not much of a reaction!" The woman smiled, and nudged herself off the side of the building, landing on her feet. "An artist likes to see her work admired. You've been looking very closely at it for quite a while."

"How long have you been watching me?" Max asked.

"Oh, you caught my attention as soon as you hollered out to graveyard girl."

Graveyard girl? "What are you talking about? Who's graveyard girl? You mean Lizzie Boggs?"

"That's right. She's the one who lives by the graveyard. Nice girl, that Lizzie Boggs."

Dizzy Lizzie lives by the graveyard? Could that girl be any weirder? Max decided to change the subject. "So you painted this mural?"

"Yep, sure did!"

Max turned around and stared at the wall for a moment. "Wait a minute... How? How can you paint anything when you're dead?"

The woman laughed. "Oh, I'll admit it wasn't easy. But where there's a will, there's a way." She waved her hand and suddenly a large hat covered with peacock feathers appeared on her head. "See?"

Max's eyes widened. "Whoa! How did you do that?"

"Trade secrets, my friend!" She grinned, then shook her head. "Oh, I'm just kidding, honey. I could tell you, but it would take forever to explain. Besides, I think you have more important things to ask me about, am I right?"

"Ask you about? What do you mean?"

"About the mural, you silly! Don't you have any questions about my work?"

"Oh!" Max looked back at the painting again. "I think I figured most of it out."

"Explain it to me, then," the woman said, crossing her arms.

Max felt like he was at school again, asked by the teacher to prove he understands the latest Algebra lesson. He was so happy to finally meet someone nice to talk with, though, he didn't care. Deciding to play along, he walked up to the left side of the mural and walked slowly to the right as he interpreted the imagery. "Well, this has to be God's hand coming out of the light over here, telling the angels to go help people on earth, right?"

Arms crossed and still smiling, the woman nodded. "You're on the right track, sweetie. Keep going."

"Okay," Max continued, "and of course this is earth in the middle. I'm guessing the living people are on this side where the light is shining on it, and the darker side is where we are, right?"

"You're doing well so far. Keep going!"

"And over here..." Max hesitated. He didn't want to talk about this part. "Over here is hell, I guess. Because it sure looks pretty nasty with all those gargoyle-looking things snarling around and grabbing people."

"Okay, well, you got the basics down. What else can you tell me about what the painting is communicating to you? There's a lot more."

Max stepped away so he could see the mural in it's entirety. "Well, it looks like the angels are trying to come to earth's rescue, because earth is being attacked by the demons."

"Some of the people on earth are being attacked, yes, but did you notice the people riding into darkness on the backs of the demons? They're not being attacked, are they?"

"Yeah, that's weird," Max said.

"Weird, why?"

"Well," Max pointed. "It doesn't make sense. Those demons are so ugly looking, and they look like they're torturing those people on earth." Max looked closer, and saw that some demons were pulling the hair of people, screaming in their ears. "You'd expect the demons to be dragging people into the darkness. But instead, it's like they..." Max stopped.

"Like they what, Max?" The woman put her hand on Max's shoulder.

"It's... almost like they... *chose* to go into the darkness. They decided that's where they want to go." Max shivered, and turned to look at the woman.

"What's happening to me, here? Am I stuck here? Am I in danger of going to hell because I didn't go with that angel into the light when I had the chance?" Max started to whimper. "What's going to happen to me?"

The woman wrapped her arms around Max, and he held onto her tight, crying in her colorful rags. "Oh, Max! Be not afraid, child. You're never stuck, you understand? People choose to stay in the In-Between for many different reasons: fear, ignorance, stubbornness, anger, denial, distrust. But others because they think there's something still here on earth waiting for them. I look at you, Max, and I see a good boy. I believe you'll be okay in the end. You just need to stay true to yourself, keep your heart pure, and you'll be all right. No boogeyman's gonna get you, you understand? You'll be tempted a lot here by the darkness, but you remember what you saw in my mural, child, and you'll be safe!"

Still clinging to the woman, Max turned his head to look at the mural again. His eyes went to that single light-colored figure on the dark side of the earth. Max released one of his arms and pointed.

"Who is that supposed to be?"

The woman let go of him to see. "Who?"

Max walked right up to the wall and pointed directly to the figure. "That one. The person who looks like he's glowing. Or she? This person looks important. It's someone on earth, but painted the same color as the other angels. Is this supposed to be Jesus? Or a guardian angel?"

"That," the woman walked up to stand beside him, "is a Lightworker."

"What's a Lightworker?"

"There are many Lightworkers here on earth. They are living people with the special ability to hear God a little clearer than most human beings. They all have different gifts. Some see or hear angels, and some just feel or know what God is telling them. Some of them are so gifted, they can even see you and me."

Max was struck by a thought. "These Lightworkers... Do they know they have these abilities?"

"No, not all of them. And some are downright confused if they're gifted enough to see the likes of you and me."

Max stared at the painting. "Why did you paint the Lightworker the same as the angels? Is it because when you see one in the In-Between, that's what they look like? They glow like angels, don't they?"

"That's right," the woman looked at Max. "You're thinking about graveyard girl, ain't you?"

Max nodded.

"I've been trying to help that girl for years, and no luck yet." She put her hand on Max's shoulder again. "If you're willing to help me get through to her, she could actually help you, Max."

Max was hopeful. All he knew at this point was that he needed to get back to the hospital so he could join his sister when the light came for her. Then he could join her, they'd be together, and he'd never have to be in this place again. "Let's do it!"

CHAPTER 5 - NIGHTMARE

Lizzie was in the middle of her best dream yet. She was sitting in the front row of a Lindsey Stirling concert. Lindsey was playing the theme on violin to one of Lizzie's favorite anime shows. After all, she had listened to it about a hundred times over before going to bed that night. Lindsey Stirling wore a red dress, and her light brown hair was loosely pinned up. Lizzie's parents bought her the meet and greet package with a special opportunity to play with Lindsey on stage! She clutched her violin in her lap and waited for the magic moment to be invited up to stage to play alongside her idol. Maybe she could even get Lindsey to sign her violin! Her palms were sweaty. *Don't be afraid*, she heard a voice say. *This is the moment you've been waiting for your whole life! You've been hiding in the shadows forever, afraid to display your gifts to the world. It's time to come out of hiding and show everyone what you're capable of doing!* Lizzie's heart raced with excitement.

"Yes!" She told herself. "This is my moment!"

Suddenly, Lindsey Stirling stopped her musical piece, lowered her violin, and looked directly at Lizzie with a great smile. "I'm so glad you're ready!" She said.

Lizzie's eyes went wide, ecstatic. But then her smile dropped. She noticed Lindsey was now wearing a gown made of colorful rags. Her hair was still pinned up loosely, but it was now black and curly.

Oh, no, Lizzie thought. *No, not now.*

Lindsey's skin color was changing now, too. And then she wasn't Lindsey Stirling at all. The woman stood on stage, hand reaching down to her, her eyes pleading. "You're ready, Lizzie, girl. Just take my hand. Everything's gonna be fine. Don't be afraid, sweetie."

Lizzie noticed a thousand eyes looking at her. She looked around and saw everyone was staring at her with hopeful eyes. Their bodies were transparent, colorless. Her heart raced, terrified.

The woman on stage tried to comfort her. "Just take my hand, girl! Take my hand. It's all good."

"No! Leave me alone! Leave me alone!" Lizzie tried to scream, but couldn't. Suddenly her conscious mind was aware that this was just a dream. She shook herself awake, and was relieved to find herself in her own room again. She sat up in her bed and looked around. Her violin was in the corner of the room, posters on the walls, and Manga books on her shelves. She breathed a sigh of relief. Weird lady gone. Hundreds of dead people staring at her... gone! Thank goodness.

Lizzie lay back down and sighed again. "Just a dream," She said aloud to calm herself. "Just a dream."

The room was dark and quiet.

And then Lizzie felt it. It was that all-to-familiar feeling that she had almost every night and every day -- the feeling that she wasn't alone.

"Lizzie?" She heard.

Her heart sped up again. She fumbled at her bedside for her

earbuds. Time to turn her music on again, to drown the sound of yet another dead person coming to her for help.

"Lizzie, c'mon! I know you can hear me."

Where are those earbuds? She was desperate.

"Lizzie! Answer me! I saw you today, and I know you saw me!"

She pressed her hands on her ears, the same way she did in the car when she heard Max yelling at her from the street.

"Stop that, Lizzie! What are you doing? Will you just answer me?"

Lizzie, eyes closed and hands pressed against her ears, finally answered. "Go away, Max! Just leave me alone!"

"What's your problem, Lizzie? You're acting like I've been bugging you all day! I just need your help with one little thing!" Max was growing angry.

"You *have* been bugging me all day, Max! All my life! Every day! Dead or alive! You and your friends – you never just leave me alone!" Lizzie's tears started again. "Will you *please*, just *leave me alone?*"

Suddenly Lizzie's bedroom door swung open, and her mother stepped into the room. "Lizzie..." She stepped over to her bed. "... Lizzie, are you okay?"

Lizzie opened her eyes. Her mom was standing over her, with Max standing directly behind. Lizzie noticed Max didn't even look at her mom. Didn't even seem to notice her mother was there. "Will you listen to me now?" He asked.

Lizzie looked at her mother. "Mom..." she started.

Max looked confused.

Lizzie continued. "Yeah, Mom. I'm okay... Sorry, I guess I was talking in my sleep again."

Her mom sat down on the bed. "Another nightmare?"

Lizzie shook her head nervously, and looked away. *Not now, Mom. I'm not talking to you in front of this kid.* "No, Mom. I don't want to talk about it."

Max was dumbfounded. He looked around the room. All he saw was Lizzie in her bed, the same glow coming from her, just as she looked when he saw her in the car. And of course mural-lady, who stayed at his side. He asked her, "Who is Lizzie talking to?"

"Oh, you can't see the living yet, son. You need more time to develop that skill."

"What do you mean? Lizzie's alive, and I can see her, fine."

The woman chuckled. "In case you didn't figure this out by now, Lizzie is one special girl."

Max shook his head, and tried to focus on the area Lizzie seemed to be talking to. Faintly he started to notice the mother's shape. She was transparent, but there. She looked like a ghost to him. Then something caught his eye from the corner of the room. He turned his head and saw it -- a dark shadowy shape.

The figure was a shape that was human-like, but very tall. It didn't move. Max started to wonder if it was just his imagination. It was very solid, unlike Lizzie's mom. Max heard Lizzie talking to her mother as he kept his gaze on the figure.

"You sure you're all right?" Lizzie's mom pressed.

"Yeah, Mom. Please, okay? I'm fine."

Lizzie's mom wasn't convinced. She frowned with concern in the darkness, turning toward the door. She wouldn't get a wink of sleep tonight. She knew Lizzie was having a hard time with the death of her dad. Lizzie had become more withdrawn than ever. It was so hard to communicate with her. The therapy didn't even seem to be helping. She had hoped it would have been helpful for Lizzie to talk to someone about her feelings – someone neutral, unbiased. But was Lizzie even opening up to the therapist? She was doubtful. She left the door cracked open as she returned to her own room across the hall.

Lizzie laid flat on her back and closed her eyes. "Please go away, Max." She whispered. "Just leave me alone." Lizzie drew her blanket over her head and gave a loud, frustrated sigh.

Max turned his gaze away from the figure. "I'll let you sleep, Lizzie," he said, "but I'm not leaving you alone until you help me."

The colorful woman held Max's arm. "Let's let her sleep, now. She needs her rest. We'll try again in the morning." She turned, walked over to Lizzie, and knelt at her bedside, looking as if she was going to say a prayer. Instead, she placed her hand on Lizzie's head. She leaned forward, almost touching Lizzie's blanket-covered head with her face. "Sleep well, Earth Angel," she said, "and may God's warriors of light protect you."

Max glanced back over to the figure in the corner again. It was gone. He looked around, but couldn't see any sign of it. He didn't get a good feeling about this dark shadowy thing. He somehow knew it was up to no good. He had the same sickening feeling that you get when you lose track of a spider in your room. It's the knowing feeling that the spider is still around somewhere, and you don't know when or where it will show up next – hopefully not up your nose in the middle of the night!

"Yeah, let's go," Max said nervously.

The woman stood, raised her head, and closed her eyes. "Have you got tonight's watch, papa?" She seemed to be asking the question to someone, but Max knew it wasn't directed to him. He looked around. Was she talking to that dark figure that mysteriously disappeared? He sure hoped not. *"Tonight's watch?"* He wouldn't want that thing watching him while he slept. Or, *"papa?"* Was she talking to God? He wondered. And why wasn't Lizzie responding to this woman at all? Could Lizzie even hear her, or feel her when she touched her head? This whole thing was so weird.

The woman smiled and nodded. Apparently someone up there answered her question. "Good," she smiled. "That girl's got the right folks watching out for her. Thank you!" She walked to Max and held his hand to lead him out. "Let her sleep in peace, son. She don't need you starin' over her all night."

The woman's words rattled inside Max's brain as he tried to make sense of them. *"May warriors of light protect you"*... *"tonight's watch"*... and who or what was that creepy shadow dude?

"Is Lizzie in danger or something?" Max winced at his own question. He had a sinking feeling that the answer to this would open a door he wasn't sure he wanted to open. There were a lot of things going on that confused the heck out of him, but maybe staying confused would be better than knowing what was really going on. Shadow people lurking in the darkness... Dizzy Lizzie his only hope, but refusing to talk to him... weird mural artist lady talking to invisible people... Did he even want to understand what was going on, here? None of this could be good.

The woman held his hand firmly. "Let's go down to the kitchen," she said. "You're gonna need a good cup o' tea for this."

CHAPTER 6 - TEA PARTY

The last thing Max expected in the afterlife was to be sitting at Dizzy Lizzie's kitchen table, having a tea party with a weird artist lady. Could this day get any more bizarre?

"One lump or two?" She reached across the little table to hand him the sugar bowl.

Max fumbled for words. "Well, um, I'm really not a fan of tea. Not hot tea, anyway." He looked helplessly at the pretty little china teacup and saucer in front of him. Dainty little rosebuds adorned the gently scalloped rim. "You wouldn't have a Coke by any chance, would you?"

The woman chuckled and handed him a can. His eyes nearly popped. The can looked to be straight out of a commercial, dripping wet as if it had just been grabbed from an ice cooler. "Seriously?" He gasped, and grabbed the can from her hands, popped the tab, and chugged it. After a few gulps, he put the can down and let out a highly satisfied, "Aaahhh!!" He wiped his mouth with his sleeve. "Man, I never thought I'd get to taste anything ever again! That was amazing!"

Max stopped, frozen, realizing this didn't make any sense at all. "How is this possible? Are you hypnotizing me or something? Ever since I got here, all I've figured out to do is how to move around without flying into the trees. How is this possible that I can actually hold something in my hand, let alone drink and taste something?"

"I guess in a way I am hypnotizing you, Max." She said. "You're not drinking that pop any more than I'm drinking this tea. I'm letting you have something that feels real... normal. Because the things I have to explain to you will be quite hard to manage, sweetie."

"But how? How can you do this?" Max looked around. It all felt so very real. He felt almost in his real body again. He felt a sense of weight again... a sense of gravity.

"I'm giving you some of my energy," she said. "That's the only way I can explain it. I'm sharing it with you. Don't expect this from anyone else you meet here. Not everyone can give away their energy like this." She smiled. "But I'm not everyone."

That's for sure, Max thought. "Hey," he realized, "I don't even know your name. Who are you, anyway?"

The woman smiled and looked down at her tea. "Took you long enough to ask! And..." She looked slyly back up at him again. "... I kinda hoped you'd never ask. I don't like to broadcast who I am on the first date, if you know what I mean."

Max gave a nervous chuckle and smiled. "Well, why not? What, are you somebody famous or something?" This woman didn't look like anyone recognizable to him. "Come on, you can tell me!"

"Ha!" She barked out a loud laugh, smiling, enjoying the moment. "No, actually I don't think I will, sweetie. It's just not the way I do things. But, hey – I tell you what. You tell me what name you want to give me, and I'll use that one, okay?"

"Oh, come on, that's silly!" Max shook his head.

"No, no!" She leaned forward. "Go ahead, now, I can take it. What's my name, Max?"

Max leaned back in his chair. "Okay, okay..." He took another gulp of his Coke. "How about..." He smiled. "... Bertha?"

The woman laughed so loud, it nearly made him fall off his chair with surprise! "Ha-ha-ha-ha! Ho!... Oh, child, you are testing me, aren't you?" She wiped the tears of laughter from her eyes. "Okay, honey." She crossed her arms and nodded. "Bertha it is!"

Max smiled. He couldn't believe how easy-going this lady was. "Okay, Bertha. So what's up, then? You're going to explain things to me, right?"

Bertha held her teacup. "I'll tell you what you need to know, and that's all. You've got some time to figure out a few things on your own, but I can see you need a little help." Her eyes lifted in the direction of Lizzie's room upstairs. "And so does that girl up there." She extended her pinkie finger from around the cup and pointed it at Max. "The two of you can help each other, Max."

"Are you kidding me?" Max's anger returned. "That dumb girl wants nothing to do with me! She won't even listen to me!"

Bertha shook her head. "That's because you're only telling her what everyone else comes to tell her, child. You want her help. I get it. But maybe you can help her first."

"Help her first?" Max scoffed. "Help her first?! Are you kidding me? I need to get to that hospital! I don't know how much time my sister has left before..." He stopped and looked down. "Before..." His voice crumbled and he broke into tears. "My little sister is dying right now!"

Bertha put her tea down, and held Max by the hand. "And there's nothin' you can do to stop that, boy. She's fighting for her own life

34

right now. You can't help her with that. That's someone else's job, you hear? But I'll tell you what you *can* do." She lifted her arm, pointing to Lizzie's room. "You can still save that girl upstairs. Millions of Earth Angels around the world are losing their light to the darkness, and you have a chance to help one right here, right now."

"Earth Angel? Lizzie?"

"Earth Angel, Lightworker, whatever the terminology. That girl is under spiritual attack, child. She needs a sense of purpose, and you need to give her that purpose. It's up to you to help Lizzie see how important she is. That's how you help her."

"Spiritual attack?" Max's mind went back to the dark figure in Lizzie's room. "That shadow thing in her room... What was that? Did you see it?"

Bertha's face was very serious. "It's always there. I have Warriors trying to protect that girl day and night. Every chance it gets, it whispers darkness in her ear, filling her mind with fears, self doubt and thoughts of worthlessness. Lizzie thinks these thoughts are her own, but she's wrong. It's like a poison these creatures inject, and it spreads like a cancer in the human soul." Bertha looked very sad. "There is nothing worse than to see people so special allow themselves to be destroyed. It's happening to millions, all over this world." She looked at Max with determination and held his hand tighter. "And we need more Warriors, Max."

Max squirmed in his seat. "Okay, well, um... I'll help with Lizzie... But I really want to get back to where I belong, and that's with my sister. Okay?"

She held his hand tenderly with both of hers. "Okay, sweetie."

CHAPTER 7 - INTERVENTION

It took a while for Lizzie to get back to sleep that night. First her disturbing Lindsey Stirling dream, and then waking up to find "Max the Ghost" in her room. What a night! Luckily she slept soundly when she finally was able to drift off.

It was a Friday morning. She awoke to her alarm and the room was still dark. School starts way too early, she thought. Because of the midnight disturbances, she barely got any real sleep. She pressed the snooze button, needing just a few more minutes under the covers.

Maybe I won't take a shower today, she thought. I need the extra time to just lie in bed. Getting out of bed was always hard for her, but even harder without a good night's sleep.

"Hey, Lizzie!" She heard. Her eyelids sprung open. She let out a whimper. It wasn't her mom's voice. *Oh, no! He's still here!*

"Hey, Lizzie! Your alarm went off. Don't you need to get up for school?"

Lizzie sneered, and pulled her covers over her head.

"Oh, c'mon! You gotta get up, Lizzie, right? Come on!"

She felt a tug on her blanket and she shrieked. "Aack! Max! Stop it! What are you doing?"

"Jeez, sorry! I'm just trying to help you."

"Max," her voice was muffled from under her blanket, "the last thing I need is your help, okay? I don't need a freaky, stupid dead kid telling me it's time to get up!" She yanked the blanket off to sit up and yell at him. "Now, leave me alo—"

Lizzie found herself in a predicament. Her mom stood in the doorway, staring at her with a very confused expression. Max was standing beside Lizzie's bed, hands on his hips, irritated, apparently unaware that her mother had just entered the room. Oh, boy, she thought, I need to improvise. She leaned over and pounded the alarm clock with her fist, and yelled at it. "Now, leave me alone, you stupid dead thingy! You dumb, inanimate object!" Lizzie winced, hoping her mom fell for it.

Mom turned to leave. "I'm making you some toast, honey. Come to the kitchen when you're dressed, okay?"

"Okay, sure, mom!" Lizzie called after her in a lilted voice. She returned to her scowl and turned to look directly at Max, speaking through clenched teeth. "Max, you go away now. I mean it."

"I can't Lizzie! I need to stay and help you. I promised I would."

Lizzie fell back down on her pillow with a thud. "Ugh! What are you talking about? Help me with *what*? I already have an alarm clock, Max. And a mom who won't let me sleep in! I don't need one more person – or dead person – bothering me! Especially in the morning!"

"Lizzie, this is not what I want to be doing either, okay? I made a promise to a crazy rag lady that I would help you out, because she says you're in danger. All I really want to do is ask for your help, but she said maybe if I helped you first, you might be willing to finally help me. Now stop freakin' complaining, Lizzie, and let's get this whole thing over with! I don't exactly like you either, you know!"

Lizzie sat up slowly. Her eyes were wide. How did Max know about the colorfully rag-dressed woman in her dreams? This black woman showed up randomly, and always seemed to have a message for her, but Lizzie never wanted to listen. Lizzie always wondered why this same woman kept popping up in her dreams. She thought it must be some character her subconscious created. *But how does Max know about her? And now this new message...* "Wait," she asked, "what do you mean, 'I'm in danger?'"

Max stammered. "Oh, um... Well, I'm not really sure how to tell you about this without scaring you too badly." Max thought for a second of the most delicate way he could put it. "But, there's a creepy shadow guy that likes to watch you sleep. He doesn't seem all that friendly. I think maybe he's the devil or something."

Max was alarmed to see that his delicate approach was not received without some sense of alarm. Lizzie clutched her blanket tight under her chin, mouth agape in a silent gasp, with wide, horrified eyes!

"Um," Max stumbled to find the right words. "I guess I should leave you alone to get dressed for school." He backed away, giving a thumbs-up. "I'll see you down in the kitchen, okay? Toast, right? Oh, yeah. Good stuff." He disappeared into the hallway and Lizzie found herself alone and terrified.

Lizzie was as pale as her mom had ever seen her when she came to the breakfast table. "Lizzie, you okay?" She checked.

Not a word. Lizzie sipped her juice.

"Well," her mom decided to try the casual approach. "TGIF, right?" She smiled.

No response. Lizzie reluctantly took a bite of toast. Her stomach was tight. "Um, mom, I'm not feeling that great. I don't think I can eat breakfast."

"Oh!" Her mom thought this must be the reason for Lizzie's strange behavior. She must be starting a stomach virus. "You wanna stay home?"

"NO!" Lizzie shouted, startling her mother. Mom's expression was alarmed. "It's just that... I mean..." She thought quickly for a save. "... We have an important test today. I don't want to miss it."

Her mom answered cautiously. Something was going on with Lizzie today. Did she really want to know what it was? "Okay, I understand. No worries. How about you lie down for a bit, then, before you head off to the bus? Might be good to rest that stomach for a bit."

Staying in that house was not an option for Lizzie. No way could she relax thinking about that devilish shadow guy lurking around. "Actually, I think I'll just head to the bus stop now." She grabbed her backpack. "I'll be okay. I just need some fresh air." She slipped her shoes on, reached for the front door, and stopped dead.

Max stood leaning beside the door, arms crossed, James Dean-style. "All right, let's go."

Lizzie looked back over at her mom who was watching her, still concerned. Lizzie smiled back at her nervously, and left the house with Max following right behind.

Lizzie spent the entire walk to the bus stop begging Max to go away. "You are NOT coming with me to school, Max!" She felt like she had a stray dog following her around. "I have enough trouble with the stupid live boys at school. Always teasing me. I don't need to give them more ammunition to fire back at me, all right? You dead people are all the same. You show up out of the blue, whenever you want. You ask me for help but you don't seem to know what you really want from me. I mean, it's like I have a big neon sign above my head that says, 'Hey! Dead people! Over here!'"

Max chuckled. "You know, you're not far off there, Lizzie."

Lizzie kept walking, but peeked at Max who followed at her side. "What do you mean?"

"Well, I sure didn't pick you out of a crowd, you know. You're not exactly the first person I wanted to come in contact with in this afterlife thing. I haven't even seen my parents yet. Truth is, you're the first live person I've been able to really see since..." Max felt weird saying it. "... since... you know..."

"Since you died." Lizzie finished. For the first time she let herself feel sorry for Max. "Well, why didn't you just try going home, Max, to see your family? Seriously, why are you hanging out with me?"

"I was on my way home when I came across Bertha. She's the one who told me to try helping you so that maybe you'd be willing to help me."

"Bertha?" Lizzie wrinkled her nose. "Who's Bertha?"

Max waved a hand dismissively. "Just some lady I bumped into, downtown, by the mural. Hey, you know she painted her own mural that totally covers the other one! It's about heaven and hell. It's actually pretty cool. She's a pretty good artist. Actually, she was in your room last night with me. She's the one who showed me where you live. You didn't see her?"

Lizzie shook her head.

"She said she's been trying to get through to you for a long time. She told me you were in danger. I think she's been trying to protect you from that bad dude in your room."

Lizzie gulped. "Is she a black lady that dresses in colorful rags?"

Max smiled, hopeful. "So you have seen her!"

"She's been visiting me in my dreams for a long time. She seems nice, but she seems to want me to do something." Lizzie frowned. "I'm afraid to know what it is. I don't think I'll like it."

"Lizzie, you should listen to her the next time she tries to talk to you. She's actually really nice. Pretty cool lady. She can make a Coke appear out of nowhere!"

"A Coke?"

"Yeah, it was, like, BAM! And there it was, in her hand! Wow, I don't know how she did it! She's really pretty awesome, Liz. Well, for a weird, dead artist lady."

Lizzie smiled and chuckled. It startled Max at first, and then he smiled, realizing this was the first time he ever saw Lizzie crack a grin.

"Max?" She asked, still walking.

"What?"

"What is it that you needed my help with?"

CHAPTER 8 - BACK TO SCHOOL

Since she left the house a bit early, Lizzie knew she had a little extra time to hang out with Max at the edge of the graveyard before heading the rest of the way to the bus stop. No way did she want the other kids to see her talking to an invisible person. "So all you need is to get to the hospital to see your sister? Really, that's it?" Lizzie was stunned. She wondered how many other dead people wanted such small favors. "Sure, that's no big deal."

"You can tell me how to get there?" Max beamed.

"Well, no, but I bet my mom could take us there. I have an idea. It'll be easy, but you'll have to wait till after school, of course."

"Oh, right." Max was so excited, he didn't want to wait. "What if you just tell your mom you're sick today? Then I could get there sooner!"

"You want me to lie to my mom? No way! Besides, she has a job. I'm not making her take off work by faking being sick, okay?"

Max wracked his brain for an idea. "How about your dad? Could he take us instead?"

Lizzie frowned and started walking again. "Goodbye, Max. I'll see you after school. Have fun hanging out in the graveyard."

"Hey, wait up!" Max followed. "How about I stick around just to make sure that shadow guy doesn't show up at school?"

Lizzie halted and looked back at him nervously. "You think he follows me to school?"

"I dunno," he shrugged. "But maybe I should stick around just to be sure. I'm surprised I can see him but you can't. I don't know what's up with that."

Lizzie looked down, and then at the small group of kids who had gathered at the corner, waiting for the ride. She sighed. "Okay, Max. *But –*" She pointed a stern finger at him. "—Don't you dare get me in trouble, Max Fletcher. If you're coming along just to mess with me, I'm not helping you! You understand? Feel free to hang around, but *no messing around*, okay?"

"Okay," Max agreed, but he had no idea what she meant by "messing around." He looked over at the corner, and was surprised to see the other kids there. It seemed that every live person looked to him like a ghost – transparent. Lizzie was the exception. In addition to the glow she had, she was also a little more solid-looking than the other living people. He noticed that he was also starting to see vehicles driving along the streets. It was getting busy now, people beginning their morning routines and commutes. But it was all still faded, as if the cars and trucks were ghosts too. I guess the longer I spend in the In-Between, the more I'm able to see the living, he thought. That made him hopeful, realizing that when he finally saw his sister, he should be able to see her quite well.

Max followed Lizzie to the small crowd. He recognized a few kids from his class at school, only one of whom he had ever spoken to before. His name was Carl Christian, and he was a bit of an odd kid.

Maybe all the strange kids in Amherst lived by the graveyard, he wondered. Carl was small for his age, and always carried an old tape recorder with him. This really made him stand out. Nobody used tape recorders anymore. Max asked Carl about it once at recess a few months ago. He said he found it in his basement one day, and that was pretty much the end of the conversation because the bell rang.

Max gave Lizzie a nudge. "Hey, maybe I'll finally find out why Carl carries around that old tape recorder." She gave him a glance and put her headphones on, determined to ignore him. He crossed his arms. "Seriously? You're tuning me out?"

Lizzie frowned at him and turned away, displaying she had no intention of acknowledging his presence around others. As annoying as it was, he had to understand. Everyone at school already thought she was nuts, he thought. Best not to give them more to tease her about.

When the bus rolled up, he followed her to her seat. She glared at him and shook her head quickly as if to say, *"Don't you dare sit next to me!"* He shrugged, and passed her, looking for an empty seat. Then he scoffed at the situation. *Hey, I can sit anywhere*, he realized. With a wide smirk, he marched to the front of the bus and sat cross-legged in the aisle, beside the driver. Lizzie leaned over to look at him and he gave her a sly wink and salute. She rolled her eyes and sunk back into her seat, turning up her music.

The bus pulled up to Amherst Junior High and Max waited by the driver to follow Lizzie out. He was starting to enjoy the fact he was invisible to everyone else. He tried poking some of the kids as they walked by him to get off the bus, and tried tugging one girl's ponytail. She actually responded and swatted the kid behind her who objected, "Hey! What was that for?!" Max laughed, quite amused.

When Lizzie passed him, she gave him a stern look, and growled through her teeth, "Stop it, Max!"

"Hey, what was that for?" He laughed again and followed her out.

Lizzie was starting to realize this could be one of the worst decisions she'd ever made, allowing Max to follow her into school. Before entering the building, she took him aside. Without looking at him, worried someone would see, she tried speaking without moving her lips. "Max, this isn't going to work."

"What do you mean?"

"Are you kidding? You're causing mischief and you haven't even entered the building yet! This is totally not okay." She gestured to him. "It's like watching the Artful Dodger entrusted with the invisibility cloak!"

Max stared at her, blankly. "Huh?"

She rolled her eyes, sighed, and walked away. "You know what? Just stay out here, okay? There is no way I want you following me around when I'm trying to pay attention in class."

Max started to follow and suddenly heard a voice calling to him from above. "Yo! Hang out with *us*, then!"

The Junior High school was two stories tall. When Max looked up to see who was speaking to him, he saw three people sitting on the edge of the roof, legs dangling. They looked like some sort of gang – all dressed in black.

"Hi, there!" Max called out.

One by one, the crew dropped off the edge of the building and landed on their feet in front of him. He could see them all in perfect detail now – two boys and a girl. It was not the kind of crowd he would normally hang out with. One of the boys wore a black leather jacket, looking like he belonged on a motorcycle. He looked the most normal out of the bunch, but his hair was slicked back, looking a bit vampire-like. The other boy had the eighties punk look going. He wore eye shadow, which looked mega-creepy, and his hair was all spiked up. His black shirt was torn at the shoulders and his lower arms nearly covered with a series of leather bracelets. The girl was the strangest of all of them. Her skin was almost a pure white, which contrasted eerily with her long black Victorian dress. She looked like she stepped out of a Tim Burton film.

This was indeed the weirdest group of people Max had ever encountered. He was about to turn away. The leather jacket guy reached over to shake his hand. "Hi, I'm Dave," he said. He seemed surprisingly normal to be hanging around with these other two.

"Um... I'm Max." Max felt significantly younger than these guys. They seemed a bit too old to be hanging around the Junior High. Realizing this made him feel even more awkward.

Dave motioned to the other two. "And those two are Carve and Stretch." He looked back at them and barked out a laugh, enjoying a private joke.

"Shut up, Dave!" The girl barked back. His voice had a snarl to it. "Ignore him. He calls me Carve, but my name's Carol." She shoved her face into Dave's. "You got that, freak? Carol!"

"And I'm Steve," growled the boy, also annoyed. "Call me 'Stretch' again, Dave, and I'll mess you up!" Dave chuckled.

Max felt very unsettled now. "What are you guys doing here? You all look too old to be at a Junior High school."

"Haha!!" Dave bellowed. "We're also too *dead* to be at school! We're not here to *learn*, kid! We're here to take what we need."

"What are you talking about?"

"We need energy, bud. The Living have plenty of it. More than they need. Come on, I'll show ya." Dave sauntered forward into the building, and Max followed. He still didn't feel a hundred percent comfortable about this guy, but he was curious to know what Dave was taking about.

Students were at their lockers in the hallways, gathering books and materials for their first class. Dave stopped by one girl who crouched on the floor. Max recognized her. She was always very quiet and shy in class. "Watch this!" Dave smirked. He grabbed one of her books and tossed it on the other side of the hallway, behind her. Unfortunately the girl didn't see what happened. But apparently he had taken the one book she needed. She searched her locker, and frantically fumbled inside her backpack.

"No!" She whimpered. "No, not again!" A strange greenish glow started to form above the girl's head, turning brighter and brighter as the girl grew quickly more and more stressed out.

Dave laughed hysterically, and moved behind her while she continued to search for her missing textbook. What happened next was startling. Dave placed his hands on the girl's shoulders and opened his mouth wide – so wide, it almost looked like Dave's face was opening up completely. His face was one big mouth. His mouth didn't actually touch the girl's head. He hovered an inch above her and it looked like he was sucking the greenish glow out of her, and into himself.

Dave stumbled away, closed his eyes, and sighed deeply, as if refreshed. "Ahh! That felt good! Man, I needed that buzz!"

The girl, still kneeling, was suddenly dazed, and stumbled to her side. Max felt the sudden urge to help her. He went to the textbook and tried to push it over to her with his hands. He felt every bit of energy surge inside him as he tried to move it. Slowly it began to shift and move across the floor, until it bumped into her back.

The girl, startled, gasped with delight when she looked behind her. The first bell rang and she grabbed the book, shoving it into her backpack.

Max felt dazed, now. "Whoa! Suddenly I don't feel so good!"

Dave pulled Max off the floor. "You need to get that energy back, pal! C'mon, there's a Social Studies test in room 107 today. Free food, man!"

Max stumbled as Dave pulled him down the hall.

Room 107 happened to be Max's own Social Studies class. He remembered dreading this class every day, and was never prepared for Mrs. Burke's Friday tests. He watched the students as they settled into their seats. The tardy bell rang, and the morning announcements commenced.

Max stared at the empty desk in the room. His seat. He looked around the room at the student faces, searching for someone who noticed he was missing. The accident only happened yesterday, so maybe people didn't know yet.

Dave piped up, hovering over one of the students. "Hey, here's a good one!" He said. "I love this kid. He never studies, and he's always stressed out! I'll let you have him, okay? I had my morning fix already."

Max shook his head slowly.

"Aw, c'mon! Look, you don't have to do anything – just stand over him and catch the rays. You need it, trust me."

Max did feel very drained, and knowing he couldn't eat or drink to give himself energy, he thought this must be the only way to get back to normal again. He frowned as he moved over to the stressed-out boy. The greenish glow was coming off him very brightly. Max extended a hand over the boy's head. He felt a strange tingling sensation. It felt electric.

Dave pushed him forward. "C'mon! You gotta get right over him to get the rush!" Max found himself forced against the boy, and it felt like someone had pushed him against an electric fence. Instinctively, he shrieked and leapt back.

Dave laughed. "Pretty narly, eh?"

"Jeez!" Max stood there, stunned. He looked around the room, noticing most people had the same glow over them, including his friends. He watched his friends for signs that they noticed he was missing, and they did seem to wonder why he wasn't there. He moved over to them to hear their conversation.

"He must be sick," he heard Eric say to Dwayne. Eric was Max's best friend. They'd hung out together since third grade, and played X-Box almost every weekend at Max's house. Dwayne hung out with them both a lot this past year, and Max had noticed Eric was starting to do a little more with Dwayne lately. They were in Band together, and Max had started Football.

"Lucky him," Dwayne said. "He's missing out on the quiz. Bet he didn't study anyway."

Max saw Eric crack a smile. He frowned. "Yeah, right – Like you guys study? Dwayne, you never got an 'A' in your life!"

"You tell 'em!" Dave called out from the other side of the room, looking for his next victim.

Max saw the girl from the hallway. *What was her name, again?* Max tried to remember. *Was it Martha? Maria? Maria, that's right!* He remembered. She looked very tired and pale. She sat farthest in the back of the room, by the windows.

Suddenly the Principal walked into the room. Max backed up, forgetting he was invisible to everyone for a second, then relaxed. The Principal gestured to Mrs. Burke and she stepped over to him, by the door. Max could faintly hear him whispering to her, his expression very serious and somber. "Oh, dear!" She gasped, touched her face, and quickly glanced over to Max's empty seat. "Thank you for letting me know," she said, her voice shaking.

As the Principal left the room, Mrs. Burke walked back to the front of the classroom. "Class, I need your attention please!"

The room hesitantly became quiet.

"I'm afraid I have some very sad news."

Max straightened to attention, amazed that he was about to witness the announcement of his own death.

"Max Fletcher was in a terrible car accident yesterday. He passed away, and his sister's in critical condition at Mercy Hospital." Gasps and whispering was heard around the room. Eric and Dwayne looked like they were in shock. "Let's have a moment of silence before class for poor Max and his family," Mrs. Burke said, calmly. "I'll get a card together for us over the weekend to sign and send to his family on Monday."

Max looked around the room and saw many shocked faces. One that particularly surprised him was Carl Christian. Carl's eyes nearly bugged out of his head. He reached into his pocket, taking out a mini notepad and scribbled something down. Max was about to move over to investigate, when he heard a noise from the back of the room.

It was Maria – *or wait, was it Mary?* – whiter than she looked before, tears streaming down her face. Max couldn't believe she was crying. He barely knew her. He saw her raise her hand, the other hand grabbing her mouth. "Mrs. Burke?" She called out weakly, as she tried to stand. "I need to go to the bathroo—" She stopped abruptly and vomited on the floor beside her desk.

There was a vast mixture of sounds coming from the class of students: gasps of surprise, moans of disgust, with a bit of laughter mixed in.

Dwayne was trying to muffle his own laughter as he blurted out,

"Oh, man! Mary just barfed!" He let out a cackle.

Mary ran from the room.

Eric raised his hand carefully. "Mrs. Burke?"

"Yes, Eric, dear." The teacher worried about what would come next. She knew Max and Eric were close. "Do you have a few words you'd like to say?"

"Well, I was just wondering," Eric smiled, hopefully. "Maybe you should cancel the test today?"

CHAPTER 9 - DEAD MEAT

Max was fuming mad. Dave noticed.

"Who's that kid over there?" Dave motioned at Eric who sat back in his seat.

"I *thought* he was my best friend," Max growled.

"Yeah, he doesn't seem too shaken up about you being dead. That sucks. This is when you really find out how people feel about you. Did you have your funeral yet? That's the biggest test of all, man! Shoot, my old man didn't shed a tear at my funeral. But I got him back good for it."

As Dave spoke, Max slowly moved over to Eric's side, fists clenched. He ended up standing right behind him and swung his fist as hard as he could at Eric's head. To Max's surprise, Eric stumbled off his seat, stunned. He cradled the side of his head with his hand and shot an angry look at Dwayne behind him.

Suppressed chuckles spread like a wave through the classroom. As Eric climbed back into his chair, he glared at Dwayne and mouthed the words, "You're dead."

Max crossed his arms and smiled proudly. Dave came up and laid an approving hand on his shoulder. "Not bad, kid!" He nodded.

Several rooms away, Lizzie was enduring her daily torture, which the school labeled P.E. Class. She was glad at least it was her first class of the day, so she could just get it over with and move on to classes that really mattered to her. The worst part of P.E. was when they had to go into the changing room before and after class to change in and out of their mandatory gear. Lizzie made sure to always wear an undershirt and pants that she wouldn't have to change, to avoid as much undressing as possible. She just knew there was someone watching in the girls' changing room. Her mom insisted she was just being paranoid and modest, but Lizzie knew better. One day she actually saw the creep who lurked in the shadows of the girls' room. He looked like an eighties punk rocker, with eye shadow and spiked hair. Of course nobody else could see him. He was one of the dead people she saw almost every week. Thank goodness he never spoke to her, and when she did see him that one day, he ran away and hid – *the coward.*

Lizzie changed her shirt quickly while the other girls chatted and gossiped. She didn't even look around for the creep anymore. She knew he was there somewhere, and that was enough. In and out. Done. Now time for her first Honors class of the day, Language Arts.

As Lizzie marched through the hallway crowd to get to her next class, she overheard mumbling from various students mentioning Max Fletcher. She slowed down her pace to overhear. *"I heard he was in a car accident... His sister's in the hospital... so terrible... can't believe it... he just made the football team."*

Lizzie kept her head down, trying to avoid eye contact with anyone, more than usual. She moved on to her next classroom and settled into her desk, pencil and notebook ready. From her seat, she could see down the hall from the open classroom door. Lizzie was surprised to see Max out by the lockers accompanied by a boy she'd noticed many times before. Her heart pace quickened. This was not good. This boy tried talking to Lizzie before, but never to ask for her help. He was not a nice ghost.

She noticed Max was also with his friends Eric and Dwayne, but of course he was invisible to them. Eric and Dwayne were apparently arguing, and Max was standing between them, arms crossed, leaning against the lockers, a sly smile on his face. The dead boy with the leather jacket looked like he was clapping and laughing, in full approval of whatever was going on.

Lizzie grabbed her pencil and went to the classroom door. The pencil sharpener was right there, so it seemed an easy excuse to get close enough to the situation to overhear what was going on in the hallway. Watching from the corner of her eye, she started sharpening.

"I didn't touch you, moron!" Dwayne yelled in Eric's face.

"Stop lying to me, Dwayne, or I swear I'll knock you on your butt!"

Max was practically sandwiched between the two boys, but he didn't seem to mind. His eyes were closed and she could faintly see a green glow happening around him. It was as if the anger of the two boys was manifesting into some kind of energy and Max was absorbing it – and enjoying it.

Just when she started to notice herself staring, she realized the leather jacket kid was looking at her. She immediately stopped sharpening and turned to go back to her desk.

"Hey, you!" The boy called out to her. She cringed and ignored him.

As Lizzie slipped back into her seat, she put all her focus on preparing her desk space for class, ignoring this ghost-boy completely.

She glanced over at Carl in the row next to her who had the old recorder out on his desk. She could hear the gears turning. Is he listening to music on that thing? Or is he recording something? She wondered. She tried focusing her attention on that quiet mechanical sound coming from Carl's tape recorder.

"Hey, Max!" Dave waved him over as he moved to Lizzie's side. "Max, check this out!"

Max didn't like to be taken away from his moment of triumph. Eric and Dwayne were about to punch each other out and Max did not want to miss it. But then he noticed Dave was standing right next to Lizzie in her class. Something inside him switched over and he rushed into the classroom. *What did Dave want with Lizzie?*

"Max, this chick refuses to talk to me. Thinks she's too good for me I guess," he grinned, and leaned his face right next to her ear. "Is that right, nerd girl? Little miss perfect, are you? Too goodie-two-shoes to talk to the big bad ghost?"

Max frowned as he watched Lizzie shift uncomfortably in her chair. "Hey, Dave, leave her alone, okay?"

Dave ignored him completely. He leaned against Lizzie's desk, practically sitting on it. Lizzie shifted her position to look away from him, remaining silent. "Did you know this one can actually see and hear us, Max? She likes to be all high and mighty. Won't even look me in the eye." He leaned over to get in her face again. "What makes you so special, girlie?!"

"Dave," Max pleaded, "come on. Let's go."

"Not until she answers my question!" Dave barked back at him, and turned back to Lizzie. "What makes you so special, huh? Huh?"

Lizzie couldn't help it. Tears started to come. "Nothing," she whispered.

"Oh!" Dave leaned closer, right up against her. "I'm sorry, what did you say, angel face?"

Lizzie spoke through clenched teeth. "Nothing. Nothing makes me special."

Dave smiled wide. "That's right, angel! And don't you forget that!"

Suddenly Dave felt a powerful shock and found himself on the floor, dazed.

Max stood over him, shouting as loud as he could. *"I told you to leave her alone!"*

Dave stumbled to his feet, dazed, energy gone. "What did you do to me?"

"Pick on her, and I'll be happy to show you again!" Max sneered. "Now leave this room and don't you ever come near Lizzie again, do you hear me?" Lizzie was still sitting at her desk, forgetting to pretend she couldn't see what was going on. She was shocked to see Max Fletcher standing up for her.

Dave pointed a firm finger at Max. "You're dead, kid!"

Max laughed. "Ha! Tell me something I don't know, Dave! And now I'll tell you something that you don't know! You ask what makes this girl so special? Well, she's a Lightworker, okay? I'm not sure what that means, but it's more special than being a stupid punk ghost kid who drains people all day long, all right? Now, go tell your dumb freako friends not to bother her anymore, or I've got more of the same to dish out to them!"

Dave had disappeared into the hallway. Max turned around, arms crossed, standing proudly next to Lizzie. She glanced up at him from her seat with a wide grin, and pointed to a note.

Max leaned over to read: *"Thank you, Max!"*

CHAPTER 10 - CARL'S RECORDER

Although being invisible felt like a sort of superpower, it wasn't much fun because the only person to laugh with was Lizzie, who was in no mood to enjoy his antics. Max mimicked the teacher's motions in front of class, stand inches from a teacher's face and stick out his tongue, or sit in the teacher's chair with his feet propped up on the desk. Nothing worked. Lizzie just buried her head and pretended not to see him through every class.

As they stood in line to board the bus back home, Max complained. "You're no fun at all, Liz."

Lizzie whispered, "I'm not talking to you, Max, until we're off the bus, okay?"

"You just make it so hard to have fun! You're way too serious, Liz. Come on, you have to admit – when I messed with Ms. Davis's whiteboard, that was pretty funny."

Liz held her flushed face in her hands, remembering. Somehow Max figured out how to switch files around within the computer. Instead of today's Algebra assignment, an enormous photograph was

displayed on the smartboard of a selfie Ms. Davis had taken at
Disneyworld with Mickey Mouse. "I can't believe you did that, Max,"
she mumbled under her breath.

"My favorite was when I kept poking Mr. Carpenter in the back.
He was so clueless. It was hilarious! He kept thinking there was
something crawling in the back of his shirt – ha!" Max laughed.

Lizzie just rolled her eyes and shook her head with disapproval.
"Thank goodness the bus is finally here," she muttered, and followed
the line to get into her seat. Max sat by the driver again, and Liz gave
him a warning glare to behave himself.

Liz put her ear buds back in and turned on her MP3 player. Peter
Gabriel again. She flipped forward to *Salisbury Hill*, and her eyes
wandered over to Carl who sat in the bench seat across the aisle, one
seat ahead of her. She always wondered about his tape recorder.
Everyone did, but whenever someone asked him about it, he would
dodge the subject. Most people thought it was creepy, wondering if he
was taping gossip to blackmail other students. But that didn't make
sense, because there was nothing secretive about carrying around a
big bulky tape recorder that looked like it came from the 1970's. If he
was secretly taping people, shouldn't he use a smaller gadget like an
iPhone? She saw Carl fumble with his bulky cassette recorder, and
placed some equally bulky headphones over his ears. Seriously,
Lizzie, thought, does this kid even know about modern technology?

Lizzie didn't realize she was still watching Carl, who was in his
own little world. She was just beginning to zone out herself,
remembering her father as she listened to one of his favorite tunes.
But suddenly she noticed Carl almost jump in his seat, grasping the
headphones on his ears, letting out a yelp! The sound and motion got
her attention, and she squinted at him curiously. Since he was across
the aisle a seat ahead of her, she could only see a portion of his face.

She saw him lean forward over the recorder and press the rewind button. His posture was intense. As he pressed play, even from her line of sight she could see that his eyes were wide as saucers as he listened and turned the volume knob up on his machine. She heard him gasp again, and rewind... again... and again... and again.

Finally Carl stopped, taking off his headphones. He took out his pad of paper and scribbled down another note. When he tucked the pad back in his pocket, he seemed to sense her looking at him. He turned his head slowly and his expression spooked her. It was the look of a person who had just discovered a great secret.

CHAPTER 11 - CARL'S SECRET

As the bus slowed to stop, Carl shoved his recorder and headphones into his backpack. He glanced over his shoulder at Lizzie Boggs who was still looking at him. Her gaze looked almost fearful. And she should be afraid, Carl thought to himself as he put his backpack on in his seat.

The bus came to a halt and Carl made a dash for the exit. He couldn't wait to get home to the privacy of his room and review the tape again. Besides, he wanted to avoid the kids from the back of the bus who were also getting off.

Keeping his head down, Carl walked swiftly down the street. He could hear the footsteps behind him as the "back of the bus" kids caught up with him. "Hey, look, it's Creepy Carl!" They said as they caught up with him.

Normally Carl would take the teasing and shrug it off when he got home. But he was still buzzing inside with excitement from his secret discovery. "Get lost!" He shouted at him over his shoulder.

The boys weren't intimidated in the least. Carl was the smallest kid in his whole grade. Back when he was in elementary school he'd been evaluated as gifted in all academic areas and was advanced from third to fifth grade. Carl supposed it sounded like a good idea to his parents, but he hated being the youngest and smallest in his class every single year. He had been placed early into kindergarten as well, so he was almost a full two years younger than anyone else in his class. While most eighth grade boys were starting to get interested in girls, Carl was still obsessed with his hobbies, and he didn't understand any of the kids around him who were well into their adolescence. He had given up long ago trying to fit in, and was content that his only friend in the world was the family cat, Winston.

The boys caught up with Carl and one of them punched him in the shoulder hard enough to leave a bruise as they trotted by. "Watch your mouth, kid!" The boy grinned as he walked past. The group laughed as they moved farther up the street, punching fists with each other.

Carl muttered under his breath in a tone only he could hear, mocking them as he watched them move further ahead of him. "Oh, yeah, congratulations. Good job picking on the scrawny kid. Major accomplishment." He smirked.

He ducked into his house – an old colonial with a large front porch. It was one of Amherst's century homes, well kept. His parents were antique dealers. They had their own shop in Historical Downtown Amherst, and they of course brought their work home with them all the time. The house was filled with antiques. Family who visited often commented that walking into their home was like a time warp into the early 1900's. The furniture was polished old wood with dark tones. Carl actually thought their house looked more like the scene from a ghost story. But maybe that was because of his personal experiences in the house.

The more antiques his parents collected, the more Carl noticed strange happenings in the house. Objects would get lost easily and then turn up in the strangest places. Footsteps and sometimes voices could be heard at night, although Carl's parents would always tell him it was just the sound of the furnace or the house settling. One day, Carl even thought he saw a ghost in the house.

But this spooky ghost stuff didn't scare Carl in the least. Instead, he was fascinated.

Carl's secret ambition was to be a ghost hunter. He couldn't wait to get his own fancy equipment someday and be the person to finally give the world proof that ghosts really exist. For now, however, at least he had an old bulky tape recorder, found in the basement. He was on cloud nine this afternoon, realizing this old tape recorder might end up doing the job! In the past, this old recorder had caught the sounds of ghostly footsteps, creaks, odd noises at night, and strange mumblings. But today this antique tool captured the Holy Grail of ghostly sounds. It recorded a voice.

Carl's parents were still away at work, and his big brother, Dirk, wasn't home yet – thank goodness. Dirk was the stereotypical high school "jock," and picked on Carl just as much as anyone else – actually, more.

Avoiding Dirk was a frequent goal. Carl hid away in his room most of the time, reading and researching his ghostly hobby. This was where Carl was headed now, practically running up the stairs to have some long-awaited solitude to review the tape again.

When he reached his room he locked the door behind him, ensuring that his big brother wouldn't barge in. He had at least an hour until Dirk got home from after-school football practice. That was good.

Carl hopped onto his bed and pulled on his headphones, ready to review the tape in private. He remembered the moment in the classroom when he decided to press record. He had taken the cue from Lizzie Boggs.

Carl could always tell when something strange was going on. But only because he was the only person in class who noticed that Lizzie Boggs was special. He had been curiously watching "Dizzy Lizzie" since he was placed into the fifth grade with her, three years ago. He watched her the way a zoologist would observe an ape's behavior, or the way a scientist would watch a rat's progress through a maze. By the sixth grade, Carl knew that either Lizzie Boggs was a psychic medium (the power to see, hear, and speak to ghosts) or else she was totally bonkers out of her mind.

After a couple years of research and observing Lizzie's behavior at school, he definitely believed she had the "gift." He brought an EMF detector to school one day, which he kept hidden under his desk on his lap. He made a point to always sit near Lizzie so he could measure the device's readings whenever he noticed her acting strangely (talking to herself, or waving away something invisible from her face). The device measured spikes of energy in the room, and whenever Lizzie acted strangely like this, the detector's readings would skyrocket. He started bringing the tape player to school for a change, and was able to record strange vocal noises around Lizzie. This was fascinating! Carl knew he was finally getting some hardcore evidence. But until today the voices were vague -- never clear.

He decided to press the record button when he looked back and noticed Lizzie Boggs was stiff as a board with tension. He figured something was up, and took the cue. He kept the machine recording until the teacher asked everyone's attention to begin. That's when he finally pressed "stop" and tucked the machine discreetly back into his backpack. He listened to the tape so much during the bus trip, he knew exactly how far to fast-forward.

Carl leaned forward, cross-legged on his bed. The recorder on his lap, he pressed the headphones tightly with both hands against his ears.

"... Nothing..." he heard Lizzie's voice say, and then some ghostly mumbling. *"... Nothing... Nothing makes me special..."* Carl hated listening to this part. He realized, Lizzie was being bullied by this mumbling ghost.

The good part was coming! He leaned forward so much, he almost curved into a ball. Eyes closed, he turned the volume up as high as it would go. There was a little more mumbling, and there it was: ***"... I told you to leave her alone!"***

Carl's eyes popped open, and grinned wide, finally free to express his true excitement. "Wow!" He sighed, loudly.

CHAPTER 12 - GRAVEYARD GAB

Lizzie was grateful that Max seemed to have lost a great deal of energy from his activities at school, so she made it home without further embarrassing incidents. When the bus pulled away, she watched Carl walk down the street, giving her a final glance over his shoulder.

She shook off the creepy feeling. I can only deal with one issue at a time, she thought to herself. First take care of the dead guy. Then deal with "Creepy Carl."

As Max followed Liz, she finally told him her plans.

"I'm going to ask my mom to take us to the hospital tonight, okay Max? She should be home from work in an hour or so. I'd text her about it, but the whole thing is so weird – I know she'll ask a bunch of questions. I may as well just wait for dinner to ask about it."

Lizzie walked past the gravestones of Amherst Cemetery with Max following at her side. "Thanks, Liz," Max said.

"I'm still not sure why you've been hanging out with me so much and not your own family," Lizzie watched her feet as they walked.

"When you first died, didn't you want to see them right away? I mean, if it was me, I'd want to see my mom and dad more than anyone."

"Of course I want to see them," Max mumbled. "It's just that... Well... I guess I'm just afraid."

Lizzie slowed her pace. "Afraid? Afraid of what?"

"I dunno." Max tried kicking the dirt at his feet. "I want to see them so badly, but... But I don't want to see them. It kinda feels the same way when I had to go visit my grandpa in the hospital before he died. I'm afraid, because I don't know how things are right now. Are they miserable? Are they angry? I almost don't want to know. I know for sure they can't be happy right now, and I don't really want to see them like that."

Lizzie listened quietly. She turned away from the road, into the graveyard and hopped up to sit on an old, worn tombstone. "Max, there's something I've been wondering about."

"Yeah?"

Lizzie tilted her head up, staring into the sky to keep the tears from escaping her eyes. "I wish my dad would visit me." Her chin wobbled and a tear fell down her cheek. "I just don't get it. People like you come to talk to me all the time. I try to ignore them, but they keep coming. There must be some way they can see that I'm able to talk to them. But there's only one person in the whole world I want to see again." Her voice broke, and she began to sob, hands wiping her face. "I've never talked about this to anyone. I miss my dad so much! Why doesn't he come see me? Do you think he's afraid too? I keep hoping that someday I'll come home and I'll see him there, waiting for me, apologizing for waiting so long to come talk to me." She began to wail. "Why doesn't he come talk to me? Why??" Her face a mess of tears, she gave her nose a long wipe with her right sleeve.

Max didn't know what to do or say. He felt totally awkward.

"Oh... Um... So your dad is dead too, then, huh?"

Lizzie looked up at Max with complete disbelief. He thought she might try to punch him. Instead she snorted out a laugh so loud, it startled him. "You are quite possibly the dumbest boy I ever met, Max!" She laughed and wiped her face dry.

Max smiled. "Come on, let's get out of this graveyard, Liz. It's too creepy."

Lizzie hopped down from her tombstone and barked out another laugh. "Ha! *You* think the graveyard is creepy, Max? *You*, the *dead guy?* That's pretty funny."

"Hey, just because I'm dead doesn't mean I belong in a graveyard, okay? Jeez, really. It's way more fun hanging around live people than dead people, trust me."

"So what's it like, anyway?" Lizzie asked, cautiously.

"What's *what* like?"

Lizzie glanced at him from the corner of her eye as they followed the sidewalk to her house. "What's it like being dead?"

Max felt a bit self-conscious at the question. He shrugged. "I dunno. Weird, I guess. I kinda keep forgetting that I don't have a real body anymore. It took me a while to figure out how to move around without flying all over the place. But I seem to be learning quickly how to do things."

"You sure are," Lizzie chuckled. "Too quickly! You really need to tone down those pranks of yours."

Max smiled, remembering the fun he had at the teachers' expense. "Okay, maybe I just got a little bit carried away."

"Ha! A *little* carried away?"

"Hey, stop giving me a hard time about it, all right? Let me have a little fun!"

"I just don't want you to end up like those other creepy ghosts at school. You seem okay, Max." Lizzie eyed him. "I just... I just hope you stay that way."

Max waved his hand at her. "Don't worry about me. I can handle myself. And I'm pretty sure I can deal with those creeps at school." Max suddenly remembered the shadowy character he saw lurking in the corner of Lizzie's room the night before. "It's that other guy I'm worried about."

"What other guy?"

"You know... That shadow guy I told you about that watches you while you sleep. I'm not sure what to do about him yet."

Lizzie closed her eyes. They finally reached the front door and she was about to unlock it to go inside. She turned the key over in her fingers, thinking.

Max grimaced. "Oh, man. Sorry, Liz. I shouldn't have mentioned it."

Lizzie stuffed the key in her pocket. "Let's just sit on the front steps, here, until Mom comes home. It's kind of nice out today, anyway."

CHAPTER 13
OPERATION: HOSPITAL VISIT

Max asked Lizzie more about her dad to help pass the time while they waited on her steps for her mom to come home. "He was really smart and funny," she smiled, remembering. "He could always make me laugh, even when I was totally depressed about something. My mom always said he could read the phone book and make it funny." She smiled bigger.

"I like hearing about your dad like this," Max said. "You seem a lot happier when you talk about the good stuff."

Lizzie looked at her feet, but kept her smile. "Yeah, there's a lot of happy stuff to remember about him. And even though he knew how to be silly, he was super smart. He taught Physics at Oberlin College. That's why we moved to Amherst in the first place. Mom and Dad said it was a really great opportunity."

"When did you move here?" Max truly couldn't remember. He lived in Amherst his whole life, and never really paid attention to Lizzie before – not until his friends started teasing her, anyway. She

69

just wasn't a girl that stood out in any way.

"I guess I shouldn't expect you to remember I've lived here since Kindergarten, Max!" She laughed. "I mean, even though we've been in the same class together every single year!"

"Jeez, stop giving me such a hard time!"

"I can't help it, Max. You make it too easy." She folded her arms, still smiling. "I mean, why is it that all that time you never noticed me and suddenly in the past couple years you and your friends started singling me out to tease?"

"Well, Liz, I don't feel bad telling you a secret I've been keeping for my so-called friends. Eric found out Dwayne had a little crush on you. That's why we started picking on you a little bit."

Lizzie jumped in her seat. "What?!"

"Haha – Yeah! I think he's into this other girl now -- Emily the cheerleader. But we sure had fun with him about that! *Dwayne and Dizzie sittin' in a tree...*" Max turned to see that Lizzie was no longer smiling.

"So that was fun, huh?" Lizzie frowned. "Teasing your friend for thinking I was someone special?"

Max grew silent, looking down at the cracked concrete steps by his feet. *Why do girls always seem to ruin a good time?*

He was relieved to finally hear the sound of an engine approaching. Lizzie's mom pulled into the driveway. "Did you lose your key again, sweetie?" Her mom asked as she exited the car and pulled a colorful purse over her shoulder.

"No, Mom," Lizzie rose from the steps. "I just thought I'd sit outside and wait for a change. It's nice enough out here."

Mom raised an eyebrow and closed the car door. "Okay, good. Any homework tonight?" Lizzie got down from the steps to give her mom space to unlock the front door. "I thought I'd heat up some leftover lasagna for us. Does that sound good?"

Max followed them inside while Lizzie went through routine conversation with her mother. He nudged Lizzie in the side as she kicked off her shoes. "Hey, Liz – You're still helping me out, right?"

Lizzie gave him the fiftieth eye roll of the day and held her hand up to shush him. She nodded to let him know the deal was still on.

"Mom, after dinner can we please go to the hospital? I need to visit someone there."

Her mom was in the kitchen already, preparing to nuke the leftover lasagna. Stunned at the request, she nearly dropped the plate. "What? Who's in the hospital?" She stared at her, concerned.

Lizzie searched for the right words. "Remember that boy I told you about who died recently? His sister was in the same accident, and she's in the hospital now. I just wanted to go say hello."

Lizzie's mother was speechless. Lizzie was such an introvert, she never wanted to go anywhere or see anyone. "I thought you told me you weren't friends with that boy who passed away."

"I'm not... I mean I wasn't..." Lizzie stammered.

"Elizabeth, what's going on?" Her mother leaned forward, against the counter. "Something is going on with you. Ever since you mentioned that boy yesterday afternoon, you've been acting very strangely. First you were crying. Then last night I heard you talking – practically yelling – in your sleep. This morning you hardly spoke a word to me and rushed out of the house, and now you're asking to go to the hospital to visit someone you barely know." She crossed her arms. "I need you to tell me what's going on. I'm very worried about you."

Lizzie went to the counter and plopped onto one of the bar stools. "Mom, I... I just need to go. I thought... I just think the family could use some support, you know? There was an announcement at school about the accident today, and I just feel really sad for the family, you know?"

Her mom smiled solemnly and came over to sit on the stool next to Lizzie. "Oh, sweetheart, I think it's wonderful for you to want to give moral support to that family. But sweetie, you've been through so much already... with Dad. I don't know if it's a good idea to put yourself in that situation."

Lizzie wasn't giving up. "That family needs someone who understands what they're going through, Mom."

Her mother sat up straight and smiled, tears forming in her eyes. "Oh, honey, I am so proud of you." She shook her head with closed eyes. "You're so much stronger than I am." She clapped her hands, and Lizzie almost jumped. "Okay, let's do it! The lasagna can wait. I'll take you straight to the hospital and we'll visit together!"

"Oh, um," Lizzie stammered, "okay!"

Lizzie watched her mother shove the leftovers back in the fridge and followed her back to the car. Max beamed with excitement and accompanied Lizzie in the back seat. As they backed out of the driveway, Mother announced: "Here we go! Operation: Hospital Visit!"

Max leaned over to Lizzie. "Your mom is kinda fun, Liz!"

"You have no idea," She smiled back at him.

CHAPTER 14 - VISITATION

While Lizzie's mom approached Mercy Hospital's front desk to get the room number, Lizzie waited with Max beyond hearing reach. "Max, I want you to know I'm going to have to ignore you as much as possible while we're here with Mom. She's already starting to get suspicious. She doesn't know I can talk to ghosts and I want to keep it that way. She's already worried about me, and forcing me to take therapy because of what happened to Dad. I don't need her thinking I'm crazy, too."

"Got it!" Max gave her two thumbs up.

Mrs. Boggs waved to her from the front desk, indicating Max's sister, Perry, was in room 317 and they followed her to the elevators. As the elevator rose, Max realized he wasn't moving up along with everyone else. The floor was moving right through him, and before he knew it, the floor was up to his armpits. Instinctively, he pushed all his energy against the floor, and was glad to see it worked to get entirely back inside the elevator. But when the elevator suddenly stopped, he kept on going through the ceiling.

"Max!" Lizzie shrieked as she watched him disappear through the ceiling of the elevator. She clapped her hands over her mouth as her mom turned to look at her.

"What?" Her mom asked.

Lizzie tried to play it cool. "That was a *max* elevator ride, Mom," she grinned as they exited the elevator to the third floor hallway.

As her mom led her down the hall to room 317, Lizzie grew increasingly self-conscious. What am I doing? She thought to herself. Max isn't even here! What am I going to say to these people? She could feel her stomach tightening.

As they approached the room, Mrs. Boggs realized she wasn't being followed anymore. She turned to see her daughter a few steps behind, holding her stomach. "Mom, I don't feel so good."

Her mother gave a heavy sigh. "I was afraid of this. It's your nerves again." She put an arm around her daughter. "Look, we'll just pop in to say hello, okay?"

"I don't know, Mom. I feel like I'm gonna be sick."

Mrs. Boggs sighed again, and looked at the open door of room 317. "Okay, I'll poke my head in and see if the family's in there. You just stay here, all right?"

Lizzie nodded. She watched her mom disappear into the room. "Max," she whispered, "where are you?"

"Stop!" Max called out helplessly, as if the word itself would do the trick. He tried grabbing the elevator cord, but it didn't work. He was just too desperate. He couldn't concentrate.

You need to calm down! Max heard a voice. It was a strong voice, and it seemed to come from all around him. *Now, concentrate and hold the cord.*

Max felt too helpless to wonder who was talking to him. He just knew the voice was right, and it gave him the encouragement he needed to find his strength enough to concentrate his energy. With all his might, he grabbed the cord to stop himself. He halted immediately. *Good job!* He heard. *Now, the elevator is going to move again. You just let go, and allow the cabin to move through your area. Don't try holding on to anything until I tell you, okay?*

"Okay," Max answered. He looked around and still couldn't see anyone. Where was that voice coming from?

The voice was right. The elevator was moving up again, and Max cringed, allowing it to move all the way through him. He looked up and saw the bottom of the cabin rise to the top floor of the hospital. "This is, like, so weird." Max muttered.

Okay, get ready! The voice prepared him. *It's coming back down now. When the cabin comes down through you again, this time you need to hold on to one of the people inside.*

Max waited and watched the elevator descend toward him. He couldn't help feeling he would get squashed by the elevator coming down on his head, but of course it just went through him. As he moved through, he saw there were a couple people inside. They looked like nurses. *Hold on, now!* The voice commanded, and Max wrapped his arms around one of them. The nurse shivered.

Finally the elevator stopped. *This is your stop,* the voice said. *Now let go of the nurse and follow her out, okay?*

Max obeyed, and was relieved to be out of the elevator. As he let go of the nurse, he heard her comment on how cold the elevator was. The other nurse shrugged. "I didn't notice anything," she said.

Max felt a hand on his shoulder and turned around to see a strange-looking man. He glowed slightly. Not as much as the angel he first met in the light, but he glowed a little more than Lizzie. He looked to be about fifty with brown hair, receding hairline and a short, graying goatee. He also wore an old gray "Genesis" band T-shirt and dark jeans. "Good job, kid," he said. "Although there's a much easier way to get around, here in the In-Between. Not sure you're ready to understand it yet, though. Hi, by the way." The man held out his hand to shake, grinning with crooked teeth. "I'm Bob."

"Oh, okay." Max shook the man's hand. "Thanks... um... Bob." He looked around. "Could you tell me the way to room 317?"

Bob laughed wide, and Max could see just how crooked his teeth were. "Seriously, kid? You can't even find the *room* by yourself?"

"Are you the elevator guy?" Max realized. His voice was the same as the voice that helped him out.

"Elevator guy?" The man laughed louder. "Elevator guy... Ha! I kinda like that. I might just adopt that title. Yeah, that was me in there, saving your butt, kid."

"Thanks for that," Max smiled. "My first time in an elevator since..."

"Since you croaked. I know." The man put his arm around Max's shoulder and started leading him down the hall. "It sucks. But hey, that's the way it goes."

"You said there's an easier way to get around. What did you mean by that?" Max asked as they strolled down the hall.

"It involves tesseracts, glomes and such. Fourth dimension mumbo jumbo. A little advanced for your adolescent mind, I think, kiddo. No offense, but you're not the brightest bulb in the pack. You've got a good heart, though, kid – and that's what counts!"

They halted suddenly, and Bob was quiet for a moment, staring solemnly ahead. Max looked and saw Lizzie curled up on the floor against the wall. "Liz!" He shouted, and ran over to her.

Lizzie's head jerked up, relieved to see him. "Max, what happened to you?"

"I got trapped in the elevator shaft. No matter, though –
everything's okay, thanks to my friend, here."

"What friend?" Lizzie asked.

Max looked behind him. Bob was still there and shook his head.
"She can't see me, kid." He said.

Max remembered Lizzie also couldn't see Bertha when they were
in Lizzie's room together. She couldn't see the dark entity that lurked
in her room, either. Max realized there was quite a lot he needed to
learn about what was going on. "I guess you can't see him," Max said.
"Too bad. He's a good guy." Max smiled at Bob.

Bob smiled back. "You go on ahead, kid. I'll wait over here for you.
I might disappear from your sight for a while, but just call me and I'll
be back so we can chat some more, okay?"

Max waved a final thank you and turned to face Lizzie who was
rising from the floor. "I feel so much better now that you're here," she
said. "I felt so stupid visiting your sister without you here. I don't
know your family at all, you know."

"I know, I know." Max looked around. "Where's the room?"

Lizzie pointed across the hall. "Mom's in there now. She's been in
there for a few minutes. I heard her talking to someone. Sounds like
your mom might be in there."

Max straightened up, suddenly afraid.

"Go on, Max," Lizzie insisted. "You've come this far. Don't chicken
out now!"

Max nodded, and marched over to room 317. He peeked in, and
saw Mrs. Boggs sitting in a chair with her arm around Max's mom.
He could see that his mom had been crying, but most shocking was to
see that she was wearing a small neck brace, and her arm was
bandaged in a sling. Her face was bruised, with a butterfly bandage
on her cheek.

Max wanted so much to hug his mom and say hello, but he knew it was no use. He turned and saw his little sister, Perry, in the bed. She looked so small in that big bed. She was only four years old. Her head and arms were wrapped in bandages. An oxygen mask covered most of her face. A machine beside the bed measured her heat rate. He could hear the faint *beep... beep... beep*.

"Oh, Perry," he sighed, wanting to hold her little hand. Sure, Perry could be a major pain, but now all he could think was how tragic it was to see her all bandaged up like this. She looked like a miniature mummy.

"You can't blame yourself, Mrs. Fletcher." Lizzie's mom tried to comfort.

Max's mom was inconsolable. "But I was the one driving. I know I didn't cause the accident, but I should never have let Max sit in the front seat. Kids are so much safer in the back. If he had been in back, he might be alive now. The car that hit us... it... it smashed right into him!" Max saw his mother break into a series of loud sobs.

I can't handle this, Max thought. I should never have come here. He turned to leave the room, and was startled to see his dad walking right into him to enter the room.

"Oh..." Lizzie's mom didn't get up. She kept her arm around Max's mother who was trying to calm herself down. "I'm Jennifer Boggs. My daughter goes to school with Max."

The room suddenly felt strange to Max. It felt like the atmosphere was thicker – as if a fog had entered the room and surrounded everyone there. Max looked around for signs of what could be causing this, and that's when he noticed it.

A dark mist was forming on the floor of the room. It was everywhere. It seemed to seep in from the shadows. It seemed to swirl around like a sick, heavy whirlwind. As it swirled, the mist slowly closed in on itself and began to form a human-like shape. Max froze in horror as he watched the thing take solid form. It was completely black, and had wings tucked away on its sides. The face was gnarled and boney. In place of eyes, there were sunken holes. The thing's teeth were black as it's skin, and looked to be inches long, curved and sharp.

Max couldn't move. He thought if he moved, the thing might notice him. Instead, he saw the thing hover behind his dad.

"Hello, Mrs. Boggs," Max's father said dryly.

It was obvious to Max that this creature was totally invisible to everyone else in the room. They paid no notice at all, but it stood so tall behind his father, it nearly touched the ceiling.

Mrs. Boggs suddenly felt very uncomfortable. "Should I leave you two alone?" She started to rise.

"No, *please!*" Mrs. Fletcher grabbed her arm. "Please stay, just for a little while."

Mr. Fletcher walked over to Perry and held her little hand. Max was surprised to see him void of any emotion. "Actually, Mrs. Boggs, I'm sorry to say, but it would be best if you left. Perry isn't supposed to have more than a couple people in here at a time. We don't want to crowd her."

"Of course," Lizzie's mom looked Mrs. Fletcher in the eyes, which were wide and desperate. "I really should go. This is really family time. Sorry for intruding."

"I'm glad you came," Max's mom smiled.

Before getting up, Mrs. Boggs scribbled something on a piece of paper and handed it to Max's mom. "This is my number. Please call if you need anything."

"I appreciate that so much," Mrs. Fletcher smiled again.

As Lizzie's mom left the room, a nurse stopped her just outside the door. "It's so nice of you to visit," she said. "You're the first relative who's been by to visit, outside the immediate family. It's such a shame what's happened to them."

"Oh, I'm not family," Mrs. Boggs said. "I don't even know the family, really. My daughter goes to the same school as their son."

The nurse cocked her head inquisitively. "How did you hear about the accident, then?"

"My daughter told me, yesterday. She was in tears on our way home from an appointment, and told me about it. So terrible." She looked back at the room. "That poor family."

The nurse looked confused. "It must have been a pretty late appointment you were driving home from."

"Not really. It started at three and was over by four."

The nurse scratched her head. "That doesn't make sense."

"Why?" Mrs. Boggs looked down the hall where Lizzie sat, still waiting against the wall, crouched on the floor. "I don't understand. Why wouldn't it make sense for my daughter to cry over a friend who died?"

"Because, ma'am, the accident happened around three-thirty yesterday afternoon. Not even the boy's father knew what happened until an hour later, and the school and relatives weren't notified until this morning."

Mrs. Boggs stared down the hall at her daughter.

"I don't mean to cause worry or concern," the nurse continued, "but there's just no way she could have known about the accident yesterday."

CHAPTER 15
DEMONS IN THE ROOM

When Lizzie's mom left the room, Max felt the heaviness return full force as the creature stood tall beside his father. His dad looked vacant to him. He was a shell of the person Max knew. Max wanted to go to his father, touch his arm and say, "Dad, I'm right here. I'm okay." But the dark creature scared him so much, he was afraid to draw attention to himself. The thing seemed to be ignoring his presence for now, and he wanted to keep it that way.

"The doctor hasn't come by yet with the MRI results," his mother said. "The nurse says he should be coming any minute, though."

"Useless doctors." His dad muttered.

The creature edged closer to his father and curled a boney, clawed hand around his shoulder. He noticed his father tense up immediately. "I can't believe you let this happen, Joyce."

His mother gasped to hear the words. "It wasn't my fault, Ted!" Max saw something move behind his mother's shoulders, and squinted. He could barely see, but there was a small creature grasping onto his mother's back. It was the shape of a small monkey, but looked more like a wingless bat because of its leathery black skin. The thing looked like it was trying to burrow into his mother's head.

"I can't believe you're blaming me," she cried. "And don't talk to me like you're the only one who's suffering here, Ted! My children are everything to me!" She gazed at her little daughter lying in the bed. "If Perry dies too, so do I. I'll have nothing left to live for!"

Max's father clenched his fists as the monster behind him held on tight. "Nothing left to live for. Okay. That's clear. I suppose that means I'm the nothing!"

"Ted – "

"No, I get it!" He wiped his brow and shook his head. "Look, I know you don't want to talk about this, but we need to start organizing Max's funeral. Your mother called and she's stepping in to help with the arrangements. She's on her way right now, and your sister's picking her up from the airport for us... You're welcome!" Max's father shook his head slowly, and gazed down at his daughter. He bent over and stroked her bandaged head.

Max noticed the monster recoil suddenly as if it had been shocked by something. A very slight glow emanated from his dad at that moment. He bent down further to kiss Perry on the head. "Bless you, our angel girl," he whispered.

The tall creature growled and grimaced, but seemed afraid to touch his father now. Max's eyes were suddenly drawn to his mother. New tears were forming in her eyes, he could see, but she was smiling now. The small creature that was clinging to her before was freaking out. It shrieked and scurried away, crawling up the wall. He could faintly see the same glow emanating from his mother as well.

"What does that glow mean?" Max allowed the words to escape his lips. "What is it?"

"It's called love," came a familiar voice behind Max.

He turned around and saw Bertha standing there, grinning.

The tall monster turned to them. It's eye holes were wide now. It gave a loud, angry shriek as its wings unfolded, nearly filling the room. Its mouth opened wide, like a creature from the deep, revealing a face filled with spiky teeth.

Bertha shook her finger at the monster. "Naughty little beast!" She scolded. "Go on, now! Shoo!"

The monster growled again in protest. It reached forward with its talons, inching closer to Max.

"Don't you touch this boy, you coward!" Bertha shoved Max behind her and stood tall between him and the beast.

The thing towered over Bertha. Saliva dripped from its teeth, mouth agape. It's wings stretched wide, creating a terrible shadow. Max saw the creature in perfect detail now. Its body was like a skeleton covered in thin, stretchy leather. He could see ribs clearly through its stretched black skin, and the face was that of a viperfish – all teeth with almost no face at all. It reached toward Bertha, looking like it would snatch her up and eat her.

"Aww," Bertha grinned. "Bless your heart!" She opened her arms wide, smiling. "Looks like somebody wants a hug!"

Bertha stepped forward with her open arms. A great white light appeared in front of her like a shield. The monster screamed. Its enormous wings flapped wildly, and as they swept the room, the creature seemed to dissipate into a cloud of dust, escaping like a whirlwind around them and out the door.

CHAPTER 16
THERE'S A WAR GOIN' ON

Bertha laughed, holding her belly. "I guess Mister Demon don't want no hug from Miss Bertha! Ha!"

"Thank goodness you came along," said Max. "Those creatures must be pure evil. It looked like they were making my parents fight with each other."

"Demons." Bertha shook her head. "Yep, that's what they do. They take advantage of human weakness. Fear, guilt, anger, depression... these things attract demons the way a sick animal attracts a predator." Bertha gazed at Max's parents. "Demons spread their poison in the world by preying on poor suffering folks like these. It's always been that way."

"You were right when you called it a coward." Max folded his arms. "Mom and dad have enough to deal with, without those nasty demon guys making it worse. So that little creature I saw bothering Mom – was that a demon too?"

"Yeah, they come in all forms and sizes." Bertha wrinkled her nose. "Nasty things. That dark figure following Graveyard Girl around – he's one o' them too, of course."

"What do they want, anyway?"

"They want what any tyrant wants, Max: power. You remember my mural, don't you?"

"Yeah." Max remembered, of course. It was hard to forget the swarm of snarling creatures crawling out from the darkness, dragging people back into the deep with them. It was horrific. He'd rather remember the beautiful side, where bright glowing people charged to earth's rescue.

"In case you haven't noticed already, sweetie, there's a war goin' on. You've experienced a lot already, I know. But I have one more bombshell to throw at you. Honey, I'm what you'd call a recruiter for this war. Do you know what that means?"

Max shrugged.

She put a hand on his shoulder. "It means, I'm on the lookout for new talent, Maxie boy. Now, I've had my eye on you since you got here, and I've seen you adapt very quickly. You also seem to have a good measure of what's right and wrong – even though you are a bit of a troublemaker at school." She let out a chuckle. "Messing with the digital whiteboard in Mrs. Davis's room?" She slapped her side. "That was a silly thing to do, son, but I gotta hand it to you, that was creative. And sticking up for Graveyard Girl against those In-Betweener bullies – I was super proud to see that!"

Max smiled. "Wow, thanks," he said. "It sure is nice to be appreciated for once. So, then – what are you recruiting for, anyway? Is it some kind of ghost club?

Bertha laughed. "Well kind of... I want to recruit you as what we call a Warrior of Light."

"A Warrior of Light? Seriously? What does that even mean?"

"Sounds high-falutin', I know. I prefer the term Light Shiners, but I was out-voted. What just happened in this room here was a good example of what we Shiners do."

"So you make that bright light appear and it makes the bad guys go away?"

"That's a pretty simple way of saying it, but yeah, basically."

Max looked at his sister in the bed. He remembered the way Perry would come up behind him and wrap her little arms around his legs. Sure, she could be a brat sometimes, but she always looked up to him. Once they role-played superheroes together. She called him "SuperMax," and the nickname stuck. "I don't know. I don't think I should be volunteering for anything like that. I need to stay here with Perry and wait for the light to come. That's why I'm here."

Bertha smiled. "No, son, that's why you *think* you're here. You've got a much bigger purpose than that."

Max felt frustration well up inside him. "What purpose? I don't have a purpose, okay? I'm dead! It's over! I died before I could even figure out what my purpose was supposed to be!"

Bertha straightened up, crossing her arms and cocking her head. "And what purpose would that have been, exactly?" Her tone was sarcastic.

Max's frustration rose higher. "I dunno. Maybe I could have been a professional football player or something."

Bertha barked out a laugh. "Oh, ho, really, Maxie? You call that purpose?"

"Hey, don't laugh at me, Bertha! That was my dream, okay? My secret dream was to be a great football player. Should I say instead that I wish my purpose could have been to be a doctor or a firefighter? Jeez, excuse me for loving sports!"

"That's not what I mean, honey." She shook her head slowly.

"You're talking about a job. A job ain't no purpose! A job's just a job."

"Okay," Max crossed his arms and shrugged. "What *is* purpose, then?"

Bertha tilted her head again, and thought for a moment. She raised a finger in the air to announce her answer. "Purpose... is who you are in the grand scheme o' things. There is no other label for it, really. Imagine you're a puzzle piece. Your purpose is to fit somewhere in a great big puzzle, made with trillions of pieces."

"Jeez," Max rubbed his head. "That sounds impossible. How can anyone really find their purpose, then?"

"You don't find your purpose, child. The purpose finds you. It finds you as you live through every phase of existence. In the body, outta the body – it doesn't matter. Your body's dead, but *you're not*, remember?" Bertha stepped closer and poked him in the chest. "You can still make choices, good or bad. And the more right choices you make, the easier your purpose can find you."

"You talk about the whole purpose thing like it really is a big puzzle. Like every little piece of that puzzle is supposed to fit into one big plan or something."

"Yeah, that's right."

"So," Max contemplated, "who makes the plan, anyway? Who designed the puzzle in the first place?"

Bertha smiled wide, eyebrow raised, and motioned upward. "The man upstairs, honey child. Who else do you think?"

Max blinked and shook his head. "What if this is all just baloney? Do I have to care about my purpose at all? What does it really matter? I'm dead anyway!"

Bertha nodded. "You're free to decide that, honey. But if you choose that way of being, you'll end up just like those In-Betweener bullies you met at school. They only care about themselves. They don't care about the harm they're doing to those poor kids. All they want is their next good energy fix. And when they drain the living, they leave them as sitting ducks for the 'bad guys" as you call 'em. Not moving toward some sense of purpose is what drives you to the dark side, Maxie. And why? A lost puzzle piece fades away and collects dust. It can be accidentally sucked into the vacuum cleaner or eaten by the dog. And trust me..." Bertha leaned closer and winked. "You don't want to end up as dog poop! That ain't no picnic, child."

Max looked at his family in the hospital room. He was suddenly hit with a thought that filled him with emptiness. "I already feel like a lost piece. What good am I to anyone now, really?"

Bertha reached out to hold his hand in both of hers. "All it takes is one lost piece to complete the puzzle," she smiled and winked again. "You are filled with love and compassion, sweetie. I see it strongly in you. You will make a great little warrior, I know it." She gestured to his parents. "And your parents need your protection, as you've seen. Demons are plentiful, and so are us warriors, but human beings are getting weaker and weaker. It's getting much harder to protect them. We need all the help we can get. We need fighters... like you, Max."

"I'm not a fighter," Max began to protest, but was interrupted by an alarm coming from Perry's heart monitor.

Max's mom shot up from her seat. "No! No!" She cried.

"Nurse! Nurse! Somebody help!" His dad yelled, running to the door.

A rush of people entered the room. Max was stunned by the sudden chaos. "What's going on?" He blurted.

Bertha held him back. She didn't say a word.

"She's arrested!" Announced the nurse.

"Perry! Perry, no!" Max cried.

A doctor began CPR while a nurse prepared the defibrillator to shock the little girl's heart back to life.

Max ran to the foot of his sister's bed. "Perry, no! Stay alive! Please! Mom and Dad need you alive! You have to fight!"

"It's charged!" The nurse rushed over with the defibrillator.

The doctor grabbed it, putting it into position. "All clear!" He yelled.

Max watched the electricity surge into his sister's lifeless body. "Fight, Perry! Fight! You have to stay alive! Fight for your life, Perry, I know you can make it!"

Suddenly Max felt a pair of little arms hug his legs behind him. He turned around slowly. There stood his little sister, bandages gone, dressed in her hospital robe.

"Perry..." Max whispered.

His baby sister gazed up and pointed at him. "*You* the fighter, Supermax!"

CHAPTER 17 - AIN'T GOT NO BODY

"Perry!" Max didn't know whether to cry or laugh. He knelt down and hugged her tight.

Perry watched the action over Max's shoulder. The doctors were frantic, and their parents kept a respectable distance. Their dad had his arm around their mother – as much as he could with her neck brace in the way. Perry pointed at them "Mommy okay?"

Max pressed his check against her little head. "Yeah," he started. Suddenly he straightened up and pushed her away, hands firmly on her shoulders, looking her in the eyes. "But Perry, you have to go back! Mom and Dad need you right now. They can't lose both of us!"

"What you mean, Max?" She looked at him, confused.

"Let me handle this," Bertha stepped in, and knelt down by the child. "Hey there, sweetie! It's time for you to go back now."

"Who you?" Perry blurted out, smiling.

"Oh, I think you know who I am, sweetie." Bertha held a hand up and placed it over Perry's face, blocking her eyes.

Perry was still and silent for a moment. Then she gasped, gave out a giggle, and smiled wide. "Oh, wow! I know you! You from my book at home!"

Bertha smiled. "Yes, dearie, but that's our little secret, okay?" She turned her head and winked at Max.

"Okay," Perry said in her bubbly voice as Bertha took her hand away. She wrapped her arms around Max. "Gotta go! You fight too, Max, okay?"

"I love you so much, Perry!" Max squeezed her and felt her fade away in his arms.

"We have a heartbeat!" One of the nurses shouted.

Max watched as he saw his parents embrace each other in the corner of the room. His mother sobbed with relief.

Max felt a gentle touch on his shoulder. "So, have you decided what to do?" Bertha asked.

"Yeah," Max sighed. "I guess so. But what if Perry's heart stops again?"

"Boy, you heard what your sister said. She wants you to fight!"

"How can she possibly know about our conversation?"

"People hear a lot when they're asleep. Who knows?"

"Well," Max thought, "I guess I'd be more use to my family if I knew how to protect them from those bad guys. Okay, it's a deal. I'll join the club."

Bertha chuckled. "Great, Maxie! Your lessons start right away."

"Lessons?" Max slouched. "Seriously? I need to go through lessons now?"

"Boy, you don't know anything yet! You need a mentor! He's waiting for you in the hallway."

"Why can't you be my mentor?"

She waved a dismissive hand at him. "Sonny, I ain't got time to be your mentor! Sheesh! Go on in the hallway. Your family's good for now. Go on!"

Max looked over at his family. Perry was still unconscious in her bed. "Are you sure it's safe to leave her alone?"

"I'll keep an eye on her, sweetie. Relax."

Max was hit with a sudden question. "Wait a minute, Perry said you looked like someone from one of her books at home. What was that all about?"

"Oh, I let her see the real me, that's all. I knew that would help her to trust what I was saying."

"The real you? You mean this..." Max gestured to her. "Your appearance is just a costume?"

"Hey, I already told you I ain't gonna tell you my real name. I ain't too fond of the name 'Bertha,' but I'll take it. It's the price I pay to keep my secret identity!" Bertha winked.

"Okay, whatever." Max gave up taking one last look at his family before leaving the room. "You promise you'll protect them until I get back?"

"Absolutely, now shoo!" She waved him on.

Max turned into the hallway. Bob was leaning against the wall, waiting patiently.

"I guess Lizzie and her mom left already, huh?"

"Yeah, they split," Bob said. "It's just you and me now, kiddo."

"So you're my mentor?"

"Oh, wow, the kid has a brain after all." Bob smiled wryly. "Come on, follow me."

"Where are we going?"

"I hate hospitals." He gave an exaggerated shiver. "Too many sick people. Let's get outta here. How about the park?"

"The park? Maude Neading Park? That's around where Lizzie lives. Pretty far from here. Lizzie's mom had to drive us."

"Oh, man, seriously kid? Jeez, I have my work cut out for me. Look... we don't need cars anymore. Cars are for moving bodies. Do you have a body?"

Max rolled his eyes. He wished he could have a less sarcastic mentor. "No," he mumbled.

Bob put a hand up to his ear and leaned forward mockingly. "What was that? I don't think I heard you. Do-you-have-a-body?"

Max slouched again. "No... I do not have a body."

"Say it again."

"I do not have a body, okay?"

"Okay, good. Just making sure. Because you sure as heck don't act like you know that. Lesson one starts now. We're leaving this establishment, but we're not *walking* out of here. And WHY is that?" Bob gestured grandly to Max for the answer.

"Because I don't have a body?"

"Whoa! Impressive!"

Max crossed his arms. He wasn't so sure he liked this Bob guy anymore.

"Now, I won't bore you with the scientific explanation of this new dimension you are now a part of. All you need to understand is that because you left your body, you are no longer a part of the third dimension. The rules of the third dimension no longer apply to you."

Max looked around himself. "But it looks like I'm still here in the hospital. I don't get it. This dimension doesn't look any different than it did before."

Bob shook his head. "Okay, new tactic. Close your eyes."

"Okay." Max obeyed.

"Can you see anything?"

"How can I see anything? My eyes are closed!"

"*Bzzzz!* Wrong! You have no eyelids! You still remember the limitations you had when you had a body. But – hey – we can use that. Now, keeping your 'eyes closed,' imagine somewhere you want to go, or a person you want to see. Someone not in this hospital."

"How about Lizzie Boggs?" Max shrugged. "She's kind of my only friend left now."

Bob softened hearing this. "Well, she's a good kid." He said, hesitantly. He furrowed his brows, knowingly. "Were you two friends in school?"

"Not really, no. Actually I wasn't all that nice to her. But we're friends now. I guess that's what counts."

"Sure," Bob seemed preoccupied with thought, but then shrugged it off. "Okay, so imagine Lizzie Boggs, then. You don't need to know where she is right now. Just picture her in your mind."

Max concentrated. "Okay."

"Now try to connect with her energy – her soul, if you will. This part might be difficult at first, so be patient. This soul is the only part of her that you can truly connect with through the dimensional plane. Do you understand?"

"I think so," Max said, as he tried hard to concentrate. Slowly he felt a strange sensation as he began to see not only Lizzie herself, but he could also see where she was. "Wow, it's working! I can see her!" Max said. "She's in the kitchen with her mom. Looks like they're finally eating those leftovers."

Bob smiled. "Good job! Now open your eyes."

When Max opened his eyes, he saw that they were actually standing in Lizzie's kitchen. "Whoa! That's amazing!" He gasped.

"You'll get the hang of it the more you practice," Bob said. "It's a very basic thing to know around here, so be sure you do practice, okay?"

"Sure," Max nodded. "Wow, this will make things so much easier!

Now I can go back to see my family whenever I want!"

Max noticed that Lizzie wasn't reacting to him. "Lizzie can still see me, right?" He asked Bob.

"Sure she can. She's just ignoring you."

"Why can't she see you? I remember she couldn't see you at the hospital."

"That's because I'm from a different dimension, kid. You'll notice I don't stick around too often. This place isn't where I belong. I made the decision to go into the light, you see."

"Oh!" Max remembered when the angel gave him the choice to go "home" into the light or to stay on Earth.

"That's right. I can see you mulling the whole thing over. When you decided to stay here, kid, you got yourself stuck in the fourth dimension. You're not a part of what people would call heaven *or* hell. You're in a place where many people get stuck, sometimes forever. When you left your body, you were visited by a representative from a dimension even higher than mine."

"This is so weird," Max was deep in thought. "How many dimensions are there, anyway?"

Bob shrugged. "Who's to know, really? I'm studying that, myself. I've been studying it most of my life – ha – and death."

"You mean you knew about these dimensions when you were still alive? How?"

"Well, I wouldn't say I knew all about them, of course. It was all just a scientific theory until I kicked the bucket and saw the whole thing was actually real. To be honest, I was an atheist when I was still in the body, like most other scientists I worked with. I believed in the theory of dimensions, but I didn't necessarily believe they had anything to do with the afterlife. Imagine my surprise."

Max scratched his head. "Wow. It all makes more sense now."

"I know it's pretty overwhelming, but it's all important information. And this knowledge will help you to better understand what I need to teach you next."

"And what's that?"

"We're on demon watch tonight, kid." He motioned to Lizzie. "That girl's in serious danger of being overtaken by the dark ones. I've been working every night to keep them away, but since you two have gotten all chummy, it would really help for you to learn skills of your own. Tonight you're going to bag your first demon."

CHAPTER 18 - LEFTOVER LASAGNA

Mrs. Boggs decided not to talk to her daughter about her conversation with the nurse in the hallway. Frankly, she still didn't know what to make of the whole thing. She realized it truly wasn't possible for Lizzie to have known about the accident in the first place. How could she have known? She wracked her brain with ideas to imagine different ways it was possible, and nothing made sense.

"Mom," Lizzie finally said, to break the ice at the dinner table, "I'm sorry for dragging us to the hospital. It really wasn't fair for me to ask you to take us there and then chicken out like that at the last minute."

"That's okay, sweetheart --" she started to say, and then cut herself off. "Wait, what do mean 'us?'"

Lizzie looked up from her leftover lasagna. "What?"

"You said, 'take *us* to the hospital.'" She leaned forward. Something was up with Lizzie. She knew it, and she was no longer interested in ignoring the signs. Lizzie had been talking to herself in her room at night often -- even yelling -- and Lizzie had insisted she was just talking in her sleep. Sometimes she would simply tell her mom she was reading one of her books out loud. It calmed her, she said, telling her it was part of the therapy. Mrs. Boggs shoved her head in the sand about this long enough, she decided. Lizzie might have a serious problem. What if she was developing schizophrenia?

"Um, I dunno..." Lizzie stammered. I must be really tired, she thought. I don't normally slip up that easily. "... I guess I just meant..." She shook her head, deciding to give the cop out answer. "I'm just tired. It's been a long, weird day."

Mrs. Boggs really didn't like pushing her daughter. For a teenager, Lizzie was a good girl. She was a little quiet and reserved, but rarely talked back and did well at school. "Okay," she gave up. "After dinner, lets both hit the hay. After your violin practice, of course."

"Sure, mom," Lizzie ate the last few bites and brought her dirty dish and fork to the sink. "Want me to do the dishes tonight?"

"No worries, I'll take care of it. You go ahead and get your practice done."

Liz nodded and went upstairs, motioning to Max *not* to follow her.

When Mrs. Boggs left the table to do the dishes, Bob and Max took their places at the kitchen table.

"Now, before we go into the war zone," Bob leaned forward, elbows on the table. "I need to explain a couple things. First, never let a demon touch you. The darkness they carry is like a virus. These things aren't just evil – they carry evil. They can spread it to anyone – even us."

Max leaned back in the chair. "I'm not sure I'm okay with this after all."

"Don't be a wuss, kid. Okay, second thing: Until I say you're ready, don't you go trying this on your own. Your girl, Bertha, tells me she sees potential in you." Bob leaned back in his chair and folded his arms, tilting his head. "Personally, I don't see it, but I've learned not to question that old girl."

"Why are you even helping me?" Asked Max. "You obviously think I'm a waste of time. Why should I listen to you?" Max slouched back in his chair, folding his arms. "I've had kind of a rough couple of days, all right? Can't you go easy on me?"

Bob sighed. "Kid, I know this is tough. You haven't even had your funeral yet. It's a lot to take in. But you decided to stay here in this dimension. It was your choice, and you need to deal with it. Look on the bright side – at least now you can learn what's really going on around here. In this dimension you can see what these people can't see. Here, you can see the enemy and learn to fight them. And speaking of which…" Bob glanced up the stairs toward Lizzie's room. "… We'd better get started." Bob rose from his chair. "Follow me."

Bob led Max up the stairs to the hallway outside Lizzie's room. "Let's wait until she's done practicing her violin. Since she can see you, she'll be upset if we go in there now. She likes her privacy."

"Do you know Lizzie?" Max asked.

Bob nodded. "Yep, I've been looking after her for quite a while now."

"So you're her guardian angel, then?"

Bob smiled and looked at his feet. "Yeah, I guess you could say that. I don't look like much of an angel, though, do I?" He gave a little chuckle.

Max chuckled in agreement. Bob was right -- he didn't look very angelic. Max imagined angels to be beautiful and elegant. Bob was neither. He just looked like a random guy you'd see lighting up a cigarette outside a gas station. Hard to believe he was a scientist in his lifetime. Max couldn't imagine this guy wearing a lab coat.

When Lizzie's violin playing stopped, her door opened. She wore plaid pajama pants and a sweatshirt with the phrase "One does not simply walk into Mordor."

"Don't judge me," she said. "You can come in now, but don't keep me awake, Max, okay?"

"Sure thing," Max agreed and stepped into the room, followed by Bob.

Max looked around, but couldn't see any demons yet. "Just so you know, Liz, I have someone here who is helping me tonight. He's like my mentor."

"I'm not 'like' your mentor, kid. I *am* your mentor." Bob interjected.

Max frowned. "And he's kind of a pain."

Lizzie seemed surprised. "Why can't I see him?"

Max shrugged. "I dunno. He says he's from a higher dimension. I guess you can only see spirits from the same dimension that I'm in right now."

Lizzie squinted. "I don't understand. If he's with you, isn't he in the same dimension? Aren't you and I in the same dimension right now?"

Bob put a hand to his forehead. "Max, you're opening a can of worms, here. Not a good time. This girl needs to go to sleep, not contemplate the structure of spiritual dimensions."

"I think it would be helpful for her to understand this whole thing," Max argued.

"Now is not the time, kid."

"Well, when is a good time?" Max threw his hands in the air.

"A time that is *not now!*" Bob's voice escalated.

Lizzie waved her hands and opened her covers to slip into bed.

"Max, I'm tired anyway, okay. I'm in no mood to lie in bed and listen to you argue with an invisible dead person in my room. You said you were going to help protect me from that demon thing, right?"

"Yeah. We'll be on night watch together, I guess. And he's not a dead person, by the way. He's a guardian angel."

Lizzie turned around and stared at Max. "Really?" She pointed, wide-eyed, and smiled. "You're talking with my guardian angel?" She reacted as if Max told her he was speaking with Elvis.

"Yeah!" Max smiled, crossing his arms proudly. "That's pretty cool, isn't it?"

"Cool?" Lizzie leaned forward. "That's not cool! That's amazing! I'm like so blown away here! I have to ask... Has he been watching over me my whole life?"

Bob nodded and Max. "He says yes," Max answered.

"Oh my gosh, I have so many questions!" Lizzie sat down on her bed.

"Tell her 'later,' okay, kid? I'm not ready to play telephone tag, here." Bob grinned.

"I think he wants to be sure you get your sleep," Max said.

"Oh, okay," Lizzie got under her covers. "Wow, my guardian angel. You know, just knowing that you're both here will help me feel..." She cut herself off, afraid to admit it to Max.

"Feel what?" Max asked.

"Safe." Lizzie smiled. She curled up under her covers, popped in her earplugs, and turned off the light on her night table. "Mom!" She called, "I'm going to sleep now!"

Max saw Mrs. Boggs enter the room and sit on the edge of Lizzie's bed. Bob wandered over and sat next to her, as if it was his nightly routine as well. "Goodnight sweetie," Mrs. Boggs kissed her daughter on the head. "God bless you and your dreams tonight. I love you."

"Love you too, Mom." Lizzie answered. "I'll be okay tonight. I promise."

Lizzie's mom gave her another kiss on the head and stroked it with her hand. "No worries, okay? I'm just down the hall if you need me."

Bob stayed seated on the side of Lizzie's bed after her mother left the room. He reached over and gently stroked Lizzie's hair. Max thought he could see tears welling up in his eyes. He leaned over and kissed her head as well. "Don't you worry, kiddo," he said as he stood up. "The kid and I will take care of things tonight."

Bob turned to Max and clapped, rubbing his hands together. "Here we go! Guard duty."

CHAPTER 19 - DEMON-FIGHTING 101

Max was still not used to the fact that sleep wasn't something he needed anymore. As he watched Lizzie fall asleep, he realized he hadn't experienced sleep for a couple days now. "Will I ever need to sleep again?" Max whispered to Bob, trying not to disturb Lizzie.

Bob knew he didn't need to whisper, but instinctively kept his voice soft as he answered. "It's ironic, actually. People always talk about death as a long-lasting sleep... but it's the exact opposite. The only reason live people need to sleep is because their bodies get tired. Sleep and rest help the body to re-energize. But us – Ha! – There's no need for us to sleep." He looked at Max. "But you and I have different ways of charging our batteries. All I have to do to recharge is return to my own dimension where I'm surrounded by all the positive energy I need. Unfortunately, kid, you've got it a little harder, here in the In-Between."

"What do you mean?"

"Well, you've met those negative spirits over at the school. They've learned how to suck the life out of the living. That's the easy way of getting energy in your dimension. Those guys are like energy vampires, basically. I need to make sure you don't take that same route. There's a better way for you to get energy without hurting living people. I suppose that brings us to the first lesson, because you'll need as much energy as possible when the spooks come after Lizzie tonight."

"Okay, I'm ready," Max said.

"Now bear with me, kid, and don't roll your eyes when I tell you this, because it'll sound a bit hokey."

"All right."

"Remember our lesson on moving from place to place by simply visualizing and connecting with the energy of a person, right?"

"Yeah, I remember. All I had to do was close my eyes and think hard about Lizzie, and I was able to actually see her, and then I saw where she was standing. Before I knew it, I was actually there with her, in her kitchen! That was totally amazing."

"Well, this is kind of the same thing. But in this case, to recharge you need to connect with the same dimension that Bertha comes from."

"Why not your dimension? Why do I need to get energy from her dimension? You said you get plenty of energy where you come from, right?"

"Yeah, but you need a more powerful energy source since you can't recharge as often or as easily as I can. All I need to do is go home. You may as well get your battery charged from the highest dimension."

"Bertha's from the highest dimension? Wow. Is she super important or something?"

Bob grinned. "You do realize 'Bertha' is just the name she let you call her, right? She's not letting you see her true identity, is she?"

"Yeah, I guess she did tell me she didn't want me to know who she really is yet." Max thought about it for the first time. "I wonder why. She does seem pretty special. She made a Coca-Cola appear out of thin air, and I was actually able to sip and taste it." Max paused in thought for a moment. "How is that even possible, anyway?"

"Well, apparently old Bertha has been performing miracles forever. Even before she kicked the bucket. That's as much as I'll tell you about it, though. I get the feeling you're on a 'need-to-know' basis where Bertha's true identity is concerned. Enough gossiping. Let's get back to business. Now, whenever you need to recharge, you think about Bertha. Close your eyes if you have to..." Bob looked at Max, expectantly.

"What?" Max leaned forward. "Now?"

"No, next winter, kid," Bob shook his head slowly. "Yeah, now!"

Max shook his own head in frustration. He didn't know how much longer he could take Bob's sarcasm. "Okay, fine."

"Eventually you'll be able to do this without closing your eyes, but since you're still used to having a body, this way will be easer for you. Okay, now imagine Bertha. See her as clearly as you can, until you can actually see her surrounded by a bright light."

Max concentrated as hard as he could. "I can see her! And I can see the light around her, too." Max could see her as if she was right above him, near the ceiling, surrounded by the light. As he concentrated more, the light grew brighter until he almost couldn't see her anymore. She seemed to dissolve into the light. "I almost can't see her, the light is so bright!"

"Wow, that's good, kid. You do learn fast. Don't worry if you can't see Bertha anymore. It's the light you need. Now reach out in front of you as if grabbing for that light."

Max followed Bob's direction and as he reached forward, the light came closer. Instinctively, Max shrunk back, worried the light would burn him.

"Don't worry, kid. Just let it happen." Bob said.

Max decided to trust, wincing with fear as the light seeped into his hands. He felt a strange tingling sensation as the light went up his arms and soon he felt himself surrounded by it.

"Excellent, kid!" Bob smiled, but changed his tone quickly as he noticed something appear in the corner of the room.

Max saw it too. It was that same dark figure he remembered seeing the first night he visited Lizzie.

"Just in time," Bob said softly.

The figure in the corner didn't move. It was the shape of a tall man, dressed in a long dark cloak. As Max stared at the thing in the darkness, he could see a hint of a face under the hood, but it was certainly not a human face. It looked to be from the same twisted family of the two demon-like creatures from Perry's hospital room. This one was more gruesome than the others. The hood obscured the eyes – if it had any. All that was left to look at under the hood was a dog-like nose and its jaws, lipless, with teeth that looked half-human, half animal. The mouth opened and it hissed at them: "She's mine!"

As if reacting to a command, a swarm of spider-like creatures the size of large rats sped out from behind the tall figure. Max shrunk back against the wall with a shriek. There must have been a hundred of these eight-legged freaks scrambling across the floor, walls and ceiling. They all headed straight for Lizzie.

Max watched in horror and disgust as the creatures swarmed over the girl's sleeping body in a matter of seconds. Bob grabbed Max by the shoulder. "Now's your chance, kid! Throw the light!"

"Wha—" Max was petrified. "What do I do?"

"Watch this!" Bob lunged to the girl's bed, forcing his arms forward. Max thought the whole scene looked like something from a superhero movie. An intense stream of light shot out from Bob, following down his arms. It blasted into the swarm of tiny beasts. The screams were deafening. The creatures hit by the blast turned to ash, producing a cloud of dust. The remaining eight-legged beasts continued to swarm over Lizzie. Max moved in a little closer to see that they were trying to burrow into her flesh.

Why doesn't Lizzie wake up? Max watched in horror.

Bob seemed to be reading his mind. "I hate these guys! They're the lowest of the low! Come on, kid! Help me blast them back to hell!"

Bob readied himself again and Max felt like he knew what to do. He could feel the energy of light surging inside him. He pushed his arms forward and yelled, "Take this!"

Max felt a buzz of energy through his core. A blast of light shot through his arms and flew from the palms of his hands like laser beams. About thirty of the spidery creatures screamed again, turning into a puff of ash.

"Yes!" Max punched the sky, victorious.

"Good work, kid!" Bob grinned, and readied himself to blast again.

"Look out!" Max shouted as he saw one of the spidery creatures heading toward Bob. Instinctively, he tried to kick it away, but as he kicked, it attached itself to his foot and started up his leg. "No! No!" Max cried out. "Help!"

Max got a closer look than he ever wanted of these creatures. The thing was definitely arachnid in shape, but with leathery skin stretched over bones. Every leg was tipped with a sharp claw, but the freakiest part was the head. The thing had enormous black eyes, pug nose, and the mouth, once again, was lipless, filled with pointed, gnashing teeth. The creature moved fast and before he knew it, the thing was climbing up to his chest. Max screamed! He could feel the thing beginning to dig itself into him.

At the sound of Max's scream, Lizzie bolted upright in her bed, removing her earplugs and blinked her tired eyes. "Max? Are you okay?"

"Hold still!" Bob yelled. Max saw him produce what looked like a dagger of light from his pocket, and poised it, ready to stab the beast on Max's chest.

Max freaked, holding out his arms to stop Bob. "Don't! No!"

Bob knocked Max's arms away with his one free hand. "I won't hurt you, you idiot! Let me kill it!"

"Max?" Lizzie, wide awake now, watched in confusion as she saw Max screaming and wrestling with an invisible person. "What the heck is going on?"

Max glanced up at Lizzie, unknowingly still under attack by the hideous little beasts. One scurried into her hair and Max watched in horror as one clawed its way behind her ear. The tall figure from the corner drew slowly nearer to Lizzie as Bob struggled to help Max.

Max distracted, Bob plunged the dagger through the arachnid on Max's chest. The thing screamed as it evaporated into a cloud of ash.

No longer concerned for himself, Max lunged toward Lizzie. "Look out!" He yelled, and shot forward another set of laser beams to kill the last of the little monsters.

"What the—" Lizzie froze. "What the heck was that, Max?"

The demon figure was at Lizzie's bedside, it's hand reaching out to touch her, hissing again. "She belongs to me!"

"That's what you think, freak!" Max stood straight as a superhero, ready to blast away again... but nothing happened. He tried again, arms stretched out. Nothing.

"You're out of juice!" Bob stepped up beside him. "But I'm not!"

The tall creature loomed behind Lizzie, who sat up, staring at

Max, confused. His talons nearly grasped her shoulders.

Bob forced his arms forward and a thick blaze of light shot out, hitting the demon in the face. The creature didn't disappear into ash like the other beasts. It winced and gave out an ear-splitting shriek. It reached out for Lizzie again.

"Max!" Bob yelled. "Tell Lizzie to grab the photograph under her pillow!"

"What?"

"Just do it!"

"Liz!" Max pointed. "There's a photograph under your pillow. Take it out!"

"How do you know --?" Lizzie was confused, but Max's voice sounded very desperate, so she did as he asked.

"Now tell her to stare at that photograph! Concentrate on it!"

"You need to concentrate on that photograph, Liz! Stare at it, okay? Trust me!"

The creature had her by the shoulders. It grinned as Max saw Lizzie's glow dissipate. Max looked at Bob, questioningly.

"It's trying to take her energy away. For Lizzie that's a very bad thing, trust me."

As the creature wrapped its arms around Lizzie, she began to cry.

"Tell her to imagine herself in the photograph!" Bob urged.

"Imagine yourself in the photo, Liz! Concentrate!" Max repeated.

Lizzie lifted the photograph and stared. Her mom took it when they visited Lakeside one summer day, a week before her dad passed away. She stood with her dad at the end of the long pier with Lake Erie behind them. She remembered the cool breeze that day, coming off the lake. Dad had his arm around her and they were laughing. It was their family custom when taking a photo to say "Cut the..." and everyone would answer "... cheeeeese!"

Through her tears, Lizzie remembered her dad's laugh as they both answered, "Cheese!" in the photo. She smiled, and held the photograph closer to her face.

"I love you Daddy," she whispered.

The creature sprung back with a shriek, as if the mere words had given it a shock. Max watched, wide-eyed, as it whisked away into the darkest corner of the room and disappeared.

All monsters gone from the room, Lizzie laid back down in bed, holding the photograph to her chest. "Can you let me go to sleep now, Max? I'm exhausted."

Max smiled, and looked over at Bob who returned a smirk. "Sure, Liz," He said. "I think you're safe for the rest of the night, but we'll be here to make sure."

"Thanks, Max," Lizzie's voice faded as she slipped quickly to sleep. "And tell my angel thank you, too, okay?"

"You just told him, yourself, Liz," Max smiled. He turned to Bob who reached out to shake his hand.

"Good job tonight, kid," Bob grinned. "Tomorrow we start the next lesson."

"Seriously?" Max slouched. "I'm feeling pretty exhausted myself!"

"That's because you let one touch you," Bob explained. "Because of that, you ran out of juice fast! You'll need to recharge again, to be sure you have energy for tomorrow."

"So, what's tomorrow's lesson, then?" Max asked.

Bob placed a hand on Max's shoulder. "Tomorrow it's your turn to be the teacher, Max. I've been waiting for someone to come along who can help my girl, here. She can't hear me, but she can hear you. And now that you know how to access the light, I need you to teach her how to do it in her own way."

"What?" Max squinted. "Lizzie's not dead, though. Why would she need to use the light? Living people recharge by sleeping and resting, right? That's what you told me."

Bob rubbed his forehead and then pointed an open hand at the sleeping girl. "So Bertha never explained to you who Lizzie is?"

Max tried to remember. He didn't know he was supposed to be taking notes. "Something about her being a Light person or something?"

Bob nodded. "A Lightworker. Lizzie Boggs is a Lightworker. It means she has the power to access the Light from higher dimensions and use it in many different ways. The problem is, she doesn't understand anything about herself yet. She knows she's different. She knows she can talk and see spirits. But she doesn't know anything else." He walked slowly over to Lizzie, looking down on her. He reached out his hand and stroked her hair lovingly. "The poor girl has no idea how special she is. That's why the dark ones are fighting so hard to get her on their side." Bob's posture stiffened. "We can't let that happen."

"What happens if they get her?"

Bob closed his eyes. "They've already gotten to her. Lizzie is depressed, lonely, and anxious. She desperately needs to understand her purpose." Bob turned his head to look directly at Max. "That's where you come in, kid."

CHAPTER 20 - THE REVEAL

The Saturday morning sun was peeking through the blinds of Lizzie's windows. Max was alone in her room. Bob left when he heard Lizzie's mom go downstairs. He said the danger was over for the night, and he wanted to see what Lizzie's mom was making for breakfast downstairs. Max thought that was weird since he wouldn't be able to eat it anyway.

Max sat on the floor, back against the wall, under Lizzie's "Attack On Titan" poster, starting to feel a little bored. As the sun brightened the room, his eyes scanned the room. You sure can get to know about a person when you look around their room, he thought. He felt he was getting to know Lizzie better than he'd ever known anyone else in his life.

As he looked around the room from where he sat, he noticed the violin propped up in the corner of her room, a few dying plants, a bookcase crammed with books and stuffed animals, and a neatly organized desk. His eyes finally landed again on Lizzie, still fast asleep. Then he noticed the photograph. It had fallen out of her grasp as she turned in her sleep and it was face-up on the floor, almost under her bed.

Max rose to his feet and wandered over. It occurred to him that he'd never actually seen a picture of Lizzie's dad, and he was curious about what this guy looked like. Since he was dead too, maybe someday he would bump into him. That would be great, he thought, because then he could take him to see Lizzie. That sure would make her happy.

"Let's see what this famous Physics professor looks like," Max said to himself as he knelt down to look at the photograph.

His head was right beside Lizzie's face, and she opened her eyes when she heard his voice. She saw Max's head right in front of her and screamed!

Max stumbled, falling on his butt, and let out a scream as well. *"What the freak, Liz?!"*

Lizzie clapped her hands to her face. "Max, oh my God, you totally freaked me out!"

"I freaked you out?" Max rose to his feet. "If I had a body, I would have peed my pants!"

Lizzie started to chuckle.

Max pointed to her. "Don't you dare laugh at me!"

"You just looked so funny when you fell down!" Lizzie couldn't contain her laughter. She bent forward and held her belly, laughing hysterically.

Max folded his arms and smirked. "Okay, laugh away. Go ahead. Laugh at the funny dead guy."

"Ho, ho, I'm sorry Max." She wiped a laughter tear from her eye. "I sure did need that, though. Oh my gosh." She sighed, trying to compose herself. "What the heck were you doing on the floor, anyway?"

"I just wanted to see your photo -- the one of your dad that you were holding last night. It fell on the floor while you were sleeping."

"Oh..." Lizzie stretched to reach down for the photograph. "It was taken on the last vacation I had with Dad. A week later he had the aneurysm."

"The what?"

Lizzie sighed. She never wanted to talk about it. "They called it a brain aneurysm. One of those weird freaky things that just happens. It's like God just flipped a switch and – poof. He was gone. No warning that anything was wrong with him. It just... happened."

"I'm sorry," Max didn't know how to react to grief. "Can I see him?"

Lizzie turned the photograph around. Max saw a proud man with a loving arm around his daughter. He smiled very happily... with a mouth of crooked teeth... and he wore a faded gray "Genesis" T-shirt.

"Oh my gosh, Liz..." Max leaned in closer and stared.

"What?"

He straightened up, and pointed to the photo. "It's Bob!"

Lizzie threw the covers off and jumped out of bed to stand in front of Max. "What? You know my dad? You've seen him?"

"He's your guardian angel, Liz! He was with me last night, teaching me how to ward off the bad guys. He's been with you all along!"

Lizzie's face was a mixture of emotions. Tears welled in her eyes, full open. Her mouth stammered to words, but nothing came out. Finally she said, "Are you sure about this?"

"Absolutely! He told me he's been with you your whole life. I never caught on to what he was really saying." Max pointed to the photo again. "That's him, all right. Same face... even the same shirt!"

Lizzie wanted to reach out and hug Max. She let out a joyful gasp and turned the photo around to look at it again. "That was his favorite shirt! I have it in a box of Dad's stuff in my closet." She let out a little chuckle. "That's amazing! He's still wearing it." She hugged the photograph, clutching it to her chest. "Oh my gosh, Max!"

He never saw Lizzie look so happy. Her glow was brighter than ever. He could feel the love and joy emanating from her like pure energy. It was so intense -- it energized him as well. Then he looked over her shoulder, and saw Bob standing in the doorway. He did not look so happy. He had the look teachers give when they catch you cheating on a test. "Max, you shouldn't have told her," he said.

Max threw his hands in the air. "Why the heck not, Bob?"

Lizzie's face lit up even more. "Bob? Max, are you talking to my dad right now?"

Bob's eyes were wide and desperate. He held his hands out. "Max, stop. Right now. We need to go downstairs. I mean it. Lizzie shouldn't say another word!"

"What? Why?"

Max saw what Bob was talking about, leaning just outside Lizzie's doorway. "Oh, no," he put his hands to his face. "How long has she been standing there?"

"Standing where? Who?" Lizzie stammered, confused. Following Max's stare, she turned around and froze. "Oh... hi, Mom."

Lizzie's mother moved out from around the corner. "Sweetheart, who on earth are you talking to in here?"

"Mom, how long have you been listening outside my room?"

"Long enough to hear an imaginary conversation with someone named 'Max' about your dad. Sweetie..." Her mother stepped forward. "Is this part of your therapy or something? It seems a strange way of working through your grief."

Thank goodness, Lizzie thought. She doesn't think I'm crazy...

yet. "Yeah, mom. I know it seems strange, but it seems to help." She was glad her mother had already come up with an explanation. Making up lies was not easy for Lizzie.

"Okay, well..." Her mom started to turn around again. "Get dressed and come downstairs, then. Breakfast is ready." She started to close the door and then stopped. "Sweetheart, I hope you know you can talk with me about things. It's hard for me too. I think we could help each other through this if you would just open up to me. It would definitely be healthier than having imaginary conversations."

"Sure, Mom," Lizzie said. "See you downstairs."

Mrs. Boggs closed the door. When Lizzie heard her footsteps fade away down the stairs, she whispered to Max, her eyes wide with excitement. "Max, tell me! Is my dad here right now?"

Max wasn't sure what to say. Bob stood at the door, motioning Max to shut his mouth. "Don't say another word to her about me, kid." He said. "I need you to leave the room with me right now. We'll talk about this in the hallway."

Max saw Bob disappear through the closed door. He began to follow and stopped, not used to moving through walls or doors yet. He turned, about to explain to Lizzie that he'd be right back, when Bob's hand reached through the closed door, grabbed his arm, and pulled him through.

While Max stood in the hallway, a little stunned, Bob began his tirade. "You idiot! How could you do that?"

"What do you mean?"

"I mean, why on earth would you tell Lizzie about me?"

"You didn't tell me not to."

"Oh!" Bob paced the floor. "Really? No wonder you're dead! Did your folks have to tell you not to stick your finger in a light socket or jump head first into an empty pool?"

Max crossed his arms. "I don't know why this is such a big deal."

"I'm not a guardian angel, Max, okay?"

"Wait... what? You're not? But you look after her."

"It gets tiresome explaining everything to you, kid. I'm not an angel! I'm a dead guy, just like you. But unlike you, nitwit, I crossed into the light. I admit, I took my time doing it, but I did it. I just wish..." Bob stopped pacing, caught in a sudden wave of emotion. "I didn't know..." Bob shut his eyes. His hands came up to cover his face. "I just wish I'd known about Lizzie's gift. I didn't know there was still opportunity to talk with her. To tell her..." He cut himself off. "But that doesn't matter now." He shook his head, hands on his hips, beginning to pace again. "You've screwed it all up, kid. How on earth do I fix this?"

"Fix what? What are you talking about? Why is it so bad for Lizzie to know you're here, watching over her? You should have seen how happy it made her! She looked like she was going to burst through the ceiling, she was so blown away!"

"She needs to let me go, you moron! I'm dead! I'm gone from her life!"

"No you're not! Don't you get it? You watch over her, protecting her every night! You hang around her house -- you even check to see what her mom's making for breakfast in the morning! You're not gone at all!"

Bob stood motionless, deep in thought.

"Maybe you're the one who needs to let go," Max said.

A little smirk grew on Bob's face, and he peered over to Lizzie's closed door. "Wow, kid," he chuckled. "I didn't know you had that in you."

"Had what?"

"Intelligence."

CHAPTER 21 - LIZZIE'S LESSON

Bob gave a deep sigh and put his hands on his hips. "Well, maybe I do need to let go, but now is definitely not the time for it. Thanks to you, my daughter knows I'm here now, and if that makes her happy, that shot of adrenaline can help her through this phase of training."

Lizzie's door suddenly opened, and Max noticed she was now wearing her dad's Genesis shirt. She smiled at him and nearly skipped downstairs to the kitchen. "Hey, now I won't be able to tell the two of you apart," Max joked at Bob as they followed her downstairs. They rested at the bottom of the stairs while Lizzie joined her mother in the kitchen.

"Morning, Mom! What's for brekkie?"

"Well, you seem to be in good spirits this morning," her mother said as she dropped a few strips of bacon onto Lizzie's plate. "Thought we could both use a treat this morning. I'm in a bacon and pancakes mood."

"Mmm..." Lizzie grabbed a strip immediately and started munching.

Mrs. Boggs was surprised by her daughter's positive attitude. She hadn't seen Lizzie like this since before her father passed away. "What has you feeling so good this morning?" She turned back to the counter to grab the plate of pancakes.

"Oh, I dunno. I guess I just had a good sleep, for once." She smiled.

"Don't think I don't notice Daddy's shirt, there." She placed the pancakes on the table, and smiled, warily. "Looks good on you."

"Yeah, this was always Daddy's favorite." Lizzie grabbed a pancake.

"Just like you," Mrs. Boggs smiled again and gave a little chuckle.

Lizzie smiled back at her mother. "Like both of us, Mom," she beamed.

Mrs. Boggs beamed back at Lizzie, feeling a wave of pure happiness wash over her. She filled her plate. "Hey, maybe you and I can do something fun today, like go see a movie. Whattaya think?"

Lizzie smiled, wondering if her dad would be with her for that as well. "Sure, Mom!"

Max approached Lizzie at the table. "Hey, Liz! Your dad and I need you for a little while this morning. There're some things he wants me to help teach you."

"Um, Mom?" Lizzie kept her positive tone.

"Yes, sweetie?"

"After breakfast, do you mind if I go out for a walk?"

"Where?"

"Oh, just out. I could just stroll around the graveyard."

"Isn't that a little... well... morbid?"

"Not at all." Lizzie crunched away her last strip of bacon. "It's quiet. I like it."

Mrs. Boggs shrugged. "All right. I'll check on what's playing while you're out there. We can do a matinee after lunch. Sound good?"

Lizzie gulped down her orange juice and wiped her face. "Yeah!" She shoved away from the table and grabbed her empty plate to put in the sink.

"You're done already?"

"Yeah, not too hungry! See you later, mom!"

"Um, okay! Say hello to the ghosts for me."

Lizzie stopped short, staring at her mom. "What?"

"I said, 'Say hello to the ghosts for me.' *You know*... in the graveyard?"

Lizzie chuckled nervously. "Heh heh... oh yeah... Good one, mom." She grabbed her jacket and waved as she scurried out the front door. "See you later!"

Down the street, Carl Christian was beginning his Saturday much less happily. Big brother, Dirk, was being a huge pain, playing his stereo at maximum volume in the room next door. Carl pounded on his brother's door. "Dirk! Turn it down! I'm working on a project!"

"It's a Saturday, dork!" Dirk called out to him. "Take a break, nerd."

Carl stomped down the stairs where his mom and dad were still eating breakfast. "Will you guys please get him an MP3 player? Every weekend he does this! I need quiet to work on my audio project!"

His mother turned around in her chair. "You know we don't want those new fancy gadgets around the house, Carl. Your father and I lived without MP3's and iPhones our whole childhood."

"So did cavemen, mom!" Carl snapped back.

"Your mom's right," his dad mumbled his usual response from behind his magazine. "If you want quiet, spend some time outside for once, son. You could use some fresh air."

"Seriously?" Carl slouched. "Fine." He stomped upstairs to his room, grabbing his recorder and a new tape. He pounded again on Dirk's door. "Neanderthal!" He shouted through the oak.

"Dork!" His brother shouted back, barely audible through the noise.

Backpack over his shoulder, Carl hurried down the stairs for the front door, slipping his shoes on. "If anyone cares to know where I am, I'll be in the graveyard... wishing I was six feet under!" He called out, and slammed the door behind him.

Lizzie hopped up on her usual tombstone. "So, what does my dad say?" She asked Max.

"About what?"

Lizzie laughed. "You said he wanted to teach me something, silly! What is it?"

"Oh, yeah." Max wasn't used to seeing Lizzie in such a good mood. She seemed like a totally different person. She was downright peppy. "He was explaining it to me while you were at the table with your mom. You saw what happened last night, right? When I blasted those spider-demons away?"

Lizzie's face dropped. "Spider-demons? What the heck?"

"Oh, don't worry, I got 'em. Hopefully they won't be back."

"Hopefully?"

Max waved his hands. "Never mind that. Time to get started with lesson stuff."

"Where's my dad right now? He's here now, right?"

Max was getting a little tired of Lizzie's distractions. "Yeah, yeah. He's standing right here with me. Please don't ask about him anymore, 'cause he's really ticked off that I even told you about him."

"He is? Why?"

"Liz, please! Can you just focus?"

"Sorry, jeez!" Lizzie slouched a little. "Okay, teach away, oh great master."

"That's the Liz I know." Max smiled. "At least I know who you got your sarcasm from. All right, now... First, Bob said, you need to ground yourself before you do this Lightworking exercise... since you're still in your body. I guess that means you should probably make sure your feet are touching the ground instead of dangling from the edge of a gravestone."

Lizzie hopped down. "Okay, now what?"

"Close your eyes, now. You have to do some imagination exercises now, and closing your eyes will make that easier."

"Okay," Lizzie did as he suggested. "No funny business, okay?"

"Now, imagine you have roots growing out of your feet. I know it sounds weird, but that's what Bob said to do. Imagine those roots are growing down from your feet, into the ground, connecting you with the earth."

Lizzie nodded, keeping her eyes closed. "I can't help but realize my roots might be intermingling with a dead person's bones. I'm standing on a grave, here, you know."

"You're distracting yourself again, Lizzie. This is just imagination, okay? The roots aren't real – they're just supposed to be real in your mind!"

"Okay, sorry! Roots coming out of my feet. Got it. Next..."

Max sighed. "Okay, I guess you're grounded, so on to step two."

As Carl reached the edge of the graveyard, he unzipped his backpack, removing his recorder. As he pulled out the new tape from his pocket, he heard someone's voice up ahead. "Oh, man," he mumbled. "I can't even get solitude *here*, of all places!" Carl stretched his neck to find where the voice was coming from. He slung his pack over his shoulder again, and tucked the recorder under his arm.

As he shifted his position, he noticed someone quite a few rows down inside the graveyard. It was that redhead girl from the bus, Lizzie Boggs. Curious, he snuck a little closer to see who was with her, but she seemed to be alone. He knelt down to hide, and strained to hear her words. She stood in front of one of the gravestones, eyes closed, with her hands stretched out in front of her, palms up. She looked like she was meditating. He remembered seeing his mother doing a similar action while practicing yoga.

"Okay, now what do I do?" He heard Lizzie say. He looked around again. Nobody there. Who was she talking to? Remembering the tape he left in his room, he wondered if the same spirit who left that recorded voice was the same spirit she was talking to now.

"Wow, I can see the light!" She said. "It's right in front of me!" He saw her reach for something invisible. She looked like she was practicing mime, now, holding an invisible beach ball in her hands.

"This girl's weirder than I thought," Carl whispered to himself. "What the heck is she doing?"

"That was amazing, Max!" Lizzie said, opening her eyes. "But I have to ask... What is this all about, anyway? Creating this bright light is pretty cool, but what's it all for? You haven't really explained that to me." She hopped up on the headstone again.

"Bob says you're a Lightworker. That means your job is to create that light for anyone who needs it. You'll need it to help yourself to fight against the demons, but the most important work you're supposed to be doing is helping lost souls find the light to get back to where they belong. Bob says that if you don't help them, they'll fall into darkness along with the demons which makes their army stronger."

"Jeez, that sounds crazy." Lizzie shook her head in disbelief.

"Your dad's words, not mine." Max held his hands up. "I can barely believe all this stuff, myself, but I've seen it with my own eyes, now. I've seen these demon things. They've made my parents argue when they should be hugging each other. And they were attacking you like crazy last night. I don't know if I'll ever forget the sight of those creepy crawly guys all over you." Max shivered. "I'm sure glad you can't see them! You'd never sleep again!"

"I don't need to hear about that again, Max," Lizzie shook her head, and noticed something move from the corner of her eye.

Carl stood up, tired of hiding. *"Max?"* He walked toward Lizzie who gaped at him. *"Max Fletcher*, the kid who died in a car wreck two days ago? You're talking to him, aren't you?"

Lizzie jumped down from the gravestone and stumbled. "What? Who?" She stammered to find words, but found herself speechless.

"Don't bother trying to come up with a lie," Carl said. "I know exactly what's going on here, Lizzie Boggs. And don't worry." He folded his arms, holding his head high. "Your secret's safe with me."

"I don't know what you're talking about!" Lizzie continued to stumble backward. She didn't know whether to run back to the house or punch this little twerp in the nose.

"Hey, I heard everything just now, and I saw your weird little pantomime exercise, whatever that was. Plus..." Carl held up the recorder. "I have it all on tape!"

"You recorded me? You little creep!" *That's it*, Lizzie decided. *I'm gonna punch this kid to kingdom come!* She marched forward, reaching for the recorder.

"No! Stop!" Carl hugged his machine. "I promise! I'll erase it! I'm not out to blackmail you! I just want to talk! You're a real, live, psychic medium! I can't believe I've actually met someone like you... and you live on my street! Holy cow, this is awesome!"

Lizzie backed down. Is this kid for real? She wondered. "I'm not that special," she crossed her arms.

"Are you kidding? That's as special as it gets! I mean, I'd give anything to have your ability! I'm wigging out here! I have so many questions!"

Lizzie held out her arms. "Hold on, Carl! Slow down! Really, I don't know you at all. I know we're in the same class, but I don't feel comfortable talking with anyone about this stuff. I'm..." she looked at her feet. "I'm a very private person."

"It takes one to know one," Carl smiled. "I'm totally private, too! Nobody at school knows that I'm into this ghost stuff. I knew if I ever told anyone what I was doing with my recorder, they'd all just think I was weird."

Lizzie chuckled. "Carl, everyone thinks you're weird anyway."

Carl chuckled in agreement. "Yeah, I know. You understand, though. People think you're weird at school, too, but you still keep your secret from them."

Lizzie smiled, realizing they had something in common after all. "Yeah, I guess you're right. We're both weird enough already. Our secrets would just give people more ammunition to throw at us, right?"

"Absolutely!" Carl smiled wide, realizing he was finally making a friend... a real friend.

Lizzie was tentative, but this Carl kid seemed genuine. Could he actually be someone to trust? "I tell you what, Carl," Lizzie said with her hand out. "You give me the tape you just recorded of me saying Max's name, and I'll trust you with my secret."

Carl opened his recorder and removed the tape. "I'll do better than that," he said. He dropped the tape on the ground and crushed it with his heel. "There!" Carl offered his hand to Lizzie. "Are we officially friends, now, Dizzy Lizzie?"

Lizzie had to admit Carl was pretty likable, and it felt great to finally trust a living person with her big secret. She took Carl's hand and shook it. "I guess so, Creepy Carl!"

CHAPTER 22 - THREE'S A CROWD

Max had been watching the scene with shock, and Bob with amusement.

"What the heck just happened?" Max stared stupidly.

Bob put an arm around Max's shoulders. "Our little dream team just got a new member, kiddo. Just in time, too, because I need to get back."

"Back? Where?"

"Back home, kid. I can't stay here too long. It drains me. I've already been here too long, but it's been necessary to teach you what you need to know to get started. And now that Lizzie's had her lesson, it's time I let you two move on to phase two."

"And what's 'phase two?'"

Bob smiled. "Time for you and Lizzie to actually use what you've been taught. You two are a team now. She takes care of the lost souls and you keep the demons at bay!" He looked over at Carl. "And our new team member..."

"Yeah, Creepy Carl. What's his purpose in all this?"

Bob shrugged. "I'm not sure yet." He smiled again. "But I have a good feeling about that kid. He's a little naïve, but he has a good, honest heart. My girl could use a friend." He nudged Max jokingly. "A friend she can actually shake hands with."

Max furrowed his brow, watching the two of them. "That better be all he does with those hands," he mumbled.

"Getting protective, are we?" Bob smirked.

Max shook his head. "Nothing. Never mind."

Bob patted him on the shoulder. "Well, I'd better get going now. Tell Lizzie I'll be back. I just need to reboot. Easier to just go home for a while. Call me if you need me. I'll be back before the funeral."

"The funeral?" Max was shocked to hear the word.

"Yes, the funeral. Your funeral, remember? It's a big day. It'll be your second chance, kid."

"Second chance? At what?"

Bob looked at Max, confused. "Hasn't anyone told you? Your funeral is your second chance to go home into the light. That's why I've been working so hard to teach you now... while you're still in this dimension where Lizzie can still see and hear you... and learn from you." Bob looked over at his daughter and smiled. "It's been wonderful to teach her more about her gift. She's really needed this. And so have I."

"I don't get it," Max rubbed his temple. "Why didn't my guardian angel tell me that the light would come again at my funeral? I thought Perry's light was my next chance... or even my *last* chance."

Bob shrugged. "Who knows why those darn angels keep so many secrets. It's like they enjoy watching us scramble through our existence, chasing our butts, trying to figure out the meaning of life and all that. I prefer direct communication. It's so much more practical. Anyway," he said, patting Max on the back, "I've gotta go. I'll see you later, kid. It's been real."

"Wait!" Max turned to stop him, but Bob was already starting to fade away. "What if I need your help?"

"Just click your heels three times!" Bob joked.

"Come on!"

Bob was almost completely faded before his last words faded with him: "Trust me, kid, you won't need me anymore. You have Lizzie. And now Lizzie has Carl. You'll all be fine."

Max stood alone, watching Lizzie wave goodbye to Carl. "See you at school on Monday!" She called after him.

"Sure thing!" Carl waved back. As he left the graveyard, he seemed just as happy as Liz.

Max watched him leave. "Well, that's great. We have a new friend, I see."

Lizzie smirked. "Now look who's being sarcastic. You're not jealous, are you Max?" She chuckled.

Max folded his arms. "You're crazy. He's a twerp. By the way, your dad left while you were saying farewell to little Carl."

Lizzie's face dropped. "What? He's gone? How could you let him leave?"

"What the heck, Liz? I'm not his keeper! He comes and goes whenever he wants, you know. Besides," Max looked down. "He said he'd be back in time for my funeral. Then I guess I can join him when the light comes back for me."

All trace of happiness on Lizzie's face was wiped away from hearing those words. "What?"

"Yeah," Max shoved his hands in his pockets, still looking down at his feet. "Not like there's anything for me to stick around for anyway. Looks like Carl's your friend, now."

Lizzie shook her head and bit her lip, trying not to cry. "You're such a jerk, Max!" She barked at him and stomped out of the graveyard. Max watched her as she marched all the way to her house and slammed the door behind her.

Max hopped up on Lizzie's favorite headstone, dangling his legs, and stayed there for the rest of the weekend.

CHAPTER 23 - COLLABORATION

That weekend, while Max sulked in the graveyard, Carl invited Lizzie over to listen to the tape he recorded that Friday at school. His parents were more than shocked to see him bring a friend over, let alone a girl.

"I want to show Lizzie the project I'm working on," he explained to them, leading Lizzie up the stairs.

"Oh, sure you do," Dirk replied with a sly smirk, leaning against the railing at the top of the stairs. He practically blocked the way with his quarterback size.

"Do you mind?" Carl said as he nudged his way past.

"Don't mind at all," Dirk winked at Lizzie as she followed Carl.

Lizzie furrowed her brows at Dirk as she walked past him. "You'd better call the zoo, Carl," she said. "Looks like one of their gorillas escaped."

Carl beamed a great smile, and nodded to his brother. Dirk returned the gesture with a sneer. Carl opened the door to his room with a grand gesture. "Welcome to my office, Miss Boggs!"

Lizzie couldn't believe her eyes. Carl's room really did look more like an office than a kid's bedroom. He had an old roll-top desk filled with drawers, each labeled. A laptop computer was open on his desk, which looked slightly out of date, but more high-tech looking than the rest of the room. She saw an interesting piece of furniture she'd also never seen before. "What's this?" She asked.

Carl was so happy to have a visitor to share his secrets with. His voice sped with excitement. "My parents are big time antique collectors and dealers. This is an old library card catalog." This piece of furniture was as large as a dresser, but was filled with at least thirty little drawers, each labeled with a metal plate and a little silver handle. "This thing is the coolest, Lizzie! Look! I have each drawer labeled chronologically." He opened one of the drawers and held out a tape. "See? All my tapes, categorized according to date!"

"Wow," Lizzie nodded slowly, not sure what to think. "That's very... organized, Carl."

While Lizzie continued to look around the room, evaluating the magazine articles he had pinned up on corkboard all over his walls, Carl took out the tape from Friday, popping it into his recorder to play it for her.

Lizzie's eyes were drawn to a poster on Carl's wall. "Hey, you like anime, too?" The poster showed a single female character with long, flowing, white hair and a pair of wings wrapped around her.

Carl looked up. "Oh, yeah, that's from an anime called 'Angel Beats.' It's about a bunch of teenagers in the afterlife world. Pretty interesting. I think you'd appreciate it. Hey, Lizzie, there's something I have to play for you!"

Lizzie turned to see Carl sitting at his desk with the recorder and a pair of headphones. "Here, put these on, Lizzie! This is what I recorded during class on Friday. It's the clearest supernatural vocal anomaly I've ever gotten. It's a super big deal!"

Lizzie put the headphones on, and Carl cranked up the volume. Lizzie heard her voice surrounded by mumblings of others in the classroom, and then finally she heard Max's voice crackle loudly as she pressed the headphones against her ears. "Wow, Carl, I didn't know it was possible for a recording device to pick up on a ghost voice."

"Really? You didn't know that?" Carl was surprised. "People do it all the time. There are paranormal societies all over the world, working with machinery ten times more sophisticated, and I can only imagine the stuff they're picking up. When I get old enough, I'm gonna get a job and buy all the equipment I need. I'm already starting to save, mowing lawns around town. Just got my first EMF detector! Wanna see it?"

"How long have you been into this stuff, Carl?" She eyed the articles spread across his walls.

"Oh, a few years now. But I've been concentrating more and more just in the past year or so. I've been looking into the hot areas of Amherst."

"Hot areas?"

"Yeah, areas with the most supernatural activity. I can't get around much since my parents still have to drive me anywhere."

"Doesn't your brother drive already?"

Carl squinted. "I think you can imagine I'd rather walk a mile in bare feet than ask my brother for a lift anywhere."

"I get it." Lizzie nodded.

"Anyway, I walk around town with my recorder and just see what I pick up. Most of the time I just get noises. Sometimes mumbling. But that voice I caught on Friday was the crown jewel!"

"It seems too much of a coincidence, Carl."

"What?"

"Well, you know. Here we are, living on the same street. You're a ghost hunter, and I'm the ghost whisperer. It's pretty amazing when you think about it."

It sure is, thought Carl. He was shocked with a sudden idea. "Hey, you and I could join forces!"

"What do you mean?"

"What I'd really love, someday, is to write my own book on ghosts, as I learn more about them, myself. With your help, I could learn so much and maybe start getting articles into some local magazines."

"Oh, I don't know, Carl."

"And I'll be sure to give you credit in any articles I get published! I could name you as my partner in research. Oh, my gosh, this is great! "

"Carl, really—"

"I know, Lizzie, I'm going a mile a minute, here. But just think about it, okay? I'll be writing all weekend, now. You go ahead home, and we can talk it over on Monday on the bus, okay? I don't want to pressure you." He stood up. "I'll see you out."

Every time Lizzie looked out her bedroom window, she saw Max sitting on that same headstone. At first she thought it was pathetic. But as the weekend wore on, she decided it was just plain ridiculous. She finally decided to approach him Sunday before nightfall.

"Aren't you going to watch over me, to protect me from those spider-demons again?" She hopped up beside him on the headstone.

"You have people watching over you. You don't need me." He said, stone-faced.

"My gosh, Max, I don't think I've ever met anyone as stubborn as you!" She hopped back down off the headstone, facing him. "Are you seriously just going to sit on this freaking gravestone forever? It's getting creepy, you know. I look out the window, and there you are, just sitting here. You haven't budged an inch since yesterday morning! It's insane."

Max shrugged. "Whatever."

Lizzie folded her arms. "Well, you might be interested to hear that your funeral service is on Wednesday. So if you're just sitting here waiting to be buried, congratulations. You only have to sit out here another three days." She turned to leave.

Max started to watch her walk back to the house, and finally called out. "I'll miss you, Liz!"

Lizzie stopped and turned to look at him. "Oh, yeah?"

"Yeah."

She shook her head. "Then why are you sitting out here like an idiot? Come on inside, Max." She smiled. "We're watching a movie." She waved her hand. "Join us, okay? Please?"

Max hopped off the gravestone. "It better not be a chick flick," he said.

CHAPTER 24
THE AMHERST PARANORMAL SOCIETY

Carl was ready at the bus stop Monday morning before Lizzie even got there. Lizzie was glad it was still dark that morning so she could talk with Carl off to the side without anyone really noticing. Max strolled along with her, having promised to behave himself at school this time.

"So," Carl was just as excited as if no time had passed since their last meeting. "Have you given my proposal any thought? Oh! Hey! Look!" He took his backpack off and took out a folded booklet. "I made it over the weekend!"

"Oh, great, show and tell," Max taunted.

Lizzie ignored Max's comment and took the booklet from Carl's hand, gazing at the cover. The initials *A.P.S.* were large at the top of the cover, and underneath was written: *Amherst Paranormal Society*. In the center of the cover was a simple drawing of a cartoon ghost with a word bubble beside it, saying "BOO!" Underneath the drawing, was written, *A record of paranormal activity in the heart of a small town. By Carl Christian and Lizzie Boggs.*

"You worked all weekend on this, Carl?" Lizzie squinted. "Nice ghost."

"Yeah, cool, right?"

"This is kinda weird, though, Carl, don't you think? I mean... what kind of 'society' do we really have with just two people? Not that I want to recruit new members."

"Well, technically we have three people, Lizzie. We have Max, too, remember? He's part of the team. I just thought it would be weird to mention him in the credits."

Max stared in shock to hear his name mentioned as part of the team.

"True," Lizzie nodded. "I don't know about this, though, Carl. I'm used to being on my own. I'm not much of a club member."

They heard the bus approaching, and Carl tucked the booklet back into his backpack. "I think you'll come around," he said. "I know deep down you're just as happy as I am about finally finding someone you don't have to hide from." He looked up at Lizzie and smiled. "It's nice to finally have a friend."

Lizzie blushed. Until this moment she wasn't sure she could really trust Carl, but it took a lot of faith and trust for him to actually come right out and call her a friend. She never met anyone at school who treated her with such acceptance. Was it possible she actually found a person at school she could fully trust?

The bus rolled up, and Lizzie smiled at him. "Come sit with me on the bus, okay, Carl? I'd love to take a look through your booklet some more."

Max decided to give Lizzie her space at school. She was ignoring him again, anyway. Besides, as soon as they arrived at school, Dave

137

and his gang approached Max. "You're not allowed here, anymore, Spencer." Dave blocked his way, sidled by Goth girl, Carol, and the punk kid, Steve.

"Who died and made you Principal, Dave?" Max smirked.

Dave's sidekicks snickered at Max's remark and Dave turned to sneer at them. They shut up immediately.

Dave turned slowly back to Max. "You seriously don't want to mess with me, squirt."

Max paused to think up a clever remark. "That's right, Dave. 'Cause you're messed up enough."

The sidekicks squirmed, trying to hold in their laughter. Dave noticed and glared at them again. He turned, taking a step toward Max. His dark figure loomed over him with clenched teeth. "I'm warning you, kid..."

"No, Dave. I'm warning you."

Dave smirked. "Oh, really?"

"That's right."

"I have plenty of power on my side, kid," Dave leaned forward. "So you'd better think twice about crossing me."

"What power is that, Dave?" Max leaned forward to challenge. "All I've seen you do is leach off the living."

Dave closed his eyes, and bent his head down. Carol and Steve glanced at each other nervously and stepped back. "Hey, Dave, careful, okay?" Steve's voice quavered.

Max heard a rustling that first sounded like wind blowing through trees. As the sound drew closer, it sounded more like the sound of a hundred flapping wings.

Max looked up and saw what looked like a flock of birds, but as it approached, he realized it was more like an army of bats... not bats... gargoyles! As the creatures settled in front of the school, some perched themselves on the edge of the roof, some settled around Dave and his gang, and some, distracted by students walking into the school building, grabbed onto them instead. Max watched in horror as the winged monsters perched atop the heads of various kids who were completely oblivious that they were being attacked. They continued to walk into the building as these creatures rode them, scratching... clawing.

It occurred to Max that just as he was being taught to channel the power of Light, Dave had mastered the practice of not only channeling, but also beckoning the Darkness and the creatures living there.

Max tried to remain composed. "Okay... So you have an army of Darkness at your disposal. Big deal."

Dave grinned, and pointed at Max, and a team of gargoyles leaped forward. They grabbed Max and began clawing at him. Max screamed. All he could hear was the terrible sound of the growling, snarling creatures, mixed with Dave's laughter.

Lizzie had just gotten inside the building when she heard Max screaming. Carl was about to leave her side when he noticed her halt. "What's the matter?" He asked.

She turned around to look outside. "I think Max is in trouble," she said.

"In trouble?" Carl wondered what kind of trouble a ghost could possibly get into. He looked around. "Where is he?"

Lizzie didn't answer. She marched quickly back out of the building, through the crowd of fellow students, craning her neck, searching for Max.

Carl followed, tugging at her arm. "Where is he? Do you see him?"

Lizzie shushed at him, still searching. Finally she saw Max. He was squirming, struggling… but against what she couldn't see. What she did see was a group of three spirits she was well familiar with. The tallest one she remembered well from last week – the ghost Max stood up against. He towered over max, laughing and taunting as the other two beside him watched, cheering.

As Max battled against the attack, he felt his energy fading. Any light he had conserved was gone. With every moment these things crawled over him, he could feel the Light energy eaten away, and the bitter darkness seeping into him. It felt like he was being injected with a type of poison. He felt sick. Finally he noticed Lizzie standing, watching helplessly.

"Lizzie!" He gasped. "Please! Help me!"

Lizzie looked around her. Most students were already in the school, but there were a few still wandering in from the buses. She desperately thought how she could communicate to Max without anyone noticing. Her heart raced. "What do I do?" She whispered under her breath.

Carl nudged her. "What's going on, Lizzie? Can I help?"

Lizzie's mind raced for a solution. "I need a diversion, Carl."

"What?"

Max wailed as one creature bit his shoulder.

"A diversion, Carl! Now! Please!"

Carl ran away from Lizzie. He knew just what to do. Standing by the entrance of the school, he raised his head, and belted out the first song that came to mind. He squatted to the beat as he pumped out the first sound affects of an ancient Charlie Drake song: "Boom yakka way-ga! Boom yakka way-ga! Boom yakka way-ga!" All eyes were on him immediately, totally confused. "In the bad-badlands of Australia, many years ago-o-o… the Aboriginie tribes were me-e-eting, a-having a big pow-wo-o-w! … Boom yakka way-ga! Boom yakka way-ga! Boom yakka way-ga!"

For a moment, Lizzie stared at Carl, wondering if he had completely gone berserk. Realizing his diversion was working like a charm, she found herself free to communicate with Max without risk of anyone noticing. "Max, how can I help?"

"The Light, Liz! Make the Light! Now! I feel like I'm dying!"

Lizzie had no idea what was going on, but she knew she had to act. Max was obviously in trouble. She remembered her lesson in the graveyard. Closing her eyes, she reached her hands in front of her, palms up, concentrating.

Dave pointed to Lizzie, directing the creatures to attack.

"Lizzie, now!" Max hollered.

A light began to form above Lizzie's hands, growing brighter and brighter, larger and larger. The creatures screeched and cowered away from her. The girl opened her eyes and looked at Max who still squirmed under attack by the grimacing gargoyles.

"Throw the light to me!" Max yelled.

She rose her arms high, holding the ball of light above her head, then threw it hard to Max.

"No!" Dave called out as the beasts screeched in pain and evaporated into a cloud of dust around Max.

"Liz!" Max stood up, finally free. "Arm yourself with the Light again! Quickly!"

Lizzie didn't question. She immediately formed another ball of light in her hands, closing her eyes, concentrating.

"Keep this one, Liz! Don't throw it away!" Max stood next to her and faced Dave and his gang. "Call your army off, you cowards!"

Dave sneered. "You haven't won anything, kid! I'm the boss around here! Me! David Black!"

"That's what you think, loser!" Max scoffed. He watched as the gargoyle creatures scurried back into the shadows. "Look at your army now, David Black! Afraid of a little light, are they? Oh, poor little demons!" Max laughed.

"I'll get you when you least expect it, kid!" Dave pointed at Max, then turned to leave with his henchmen.

Max and Lizzie turned at the sound of a ruckus going on at the entrance of the school. Assistant Principal Johnson was breaking up Carl's musical diversion. "What on earth is going on, here?" Ms. Johnson didn't know whether to smile or frown.

Carl shrugged. "I just felt a song coming on! You know, sometimes you just gotta seize the moment when inspiration hits you. Right, Ms. Johnson?"

"I wouldn't know." She folded her arms, and raised her head to speak to the crowd. "All right, everyone! Show's over! Go to your classes! First bell's about to ring!" She looked at Carl. "You rarely cause trouble, young man, so I'll let you off with a warning this time. I'll be calling your folks, though, about this. I can't have disruptions from you anymore."

"I understand, Ma'am. It'll never happen again, I promise." Carl held his hand to his chest as he walked back into the school. He looked over his shoulder at Lizzie in the distance who gave him a thankful smile. He sent her a little salute in response.

The remainder of the day was a typical Monday, until Carl visited his locker to fetch his workbook for Algebra class. As he approached, he found a note tightly folded and wedged into his locker door. Carl's guard instinctively was up. The only notes anyone had ever left him before would read: "nerd, dork" and any number of profane statements. Pulling out the folded piece of paper, he smiled wide to see writing on the outside: "A.P.S. Official Secret Business."

He looked around, feeling like a secret agent as he unfolded the note. He squinted at Lizzie's almost microscopic handwriting:

Creepy Carl,

I need you to investigate the name "David Black."

Teenager who might have died back in the 1950's.

Sincerely, Diz Liz.

CHAPTER 25
FINDING DAVID BLACK

The following morning was unusually quiet. No smart remarks or antics from Max. Lizzie was wondering what was up. "Are you okay? She asked him when they left the house that morning to head to the bus for another day at school.

"Tomorrow's my funeral." Max said. "Your dad told me that's when I'll get my second chance."

"Second chance at what?" Lizzie asked.

"To choose to go into the light... like I was supposed to do in the first place."

"Oh," Lizzie looked down as they continued to walk.

Max glanced at her. "I guess you'll be happy to see me go, right?"

Lizzie smiled and shrugged. "Well, I don't know about that."

"Yeah?"

"I guess I'm getting used to having you around. I'm..." She stopped walking, staring down at the sidewalk in front of her.

"What, Liz?"

Lizzie raised her head and looked him in the face. His face was gentle and kind – not the face of the Max Fletcher she remembered from before the accident. She saw how he had changed, in such a short period of time. Or maybe it wasn't how he changed. The way he looked at her was different from before. She saw in his face now that he trusted her completely... even respected her. She never saw anyone look at her that way before. Not since her father died.

"I'm... going to miss you, Max." She said. She felt tears start to well up in her eyes, and quickly blinked them away. "Even though you are a bit of a pain." She added.

Max laughed. "Yeah, I've gotten pretty used to you too, Liz." He was surprised to realize that Lizzie was becoming the truest friend he ever had. Most kids at school seemed to always want to be close to him just to be part of the "in" crowd, or to keep from being bullied. Lizzie was different. Of course being on the football team or being part of the "in" crowd didn't matter anymore, now that he was dead. All that mattered was being himself. Max was finally starting to realize what that actually meant.

Before Max had a chance to express anything further to Lizzie, Carl ran up to them, out of breath. "Hey, Diz!" He panted. "Oh, wait – You don't mind me calling you 'Diz,' do you?" Carl always wanted a friend he could give a nickname to.

"All right, 'Creep!'" Lizzie smiled and leaned toward him to show she was just teasing.

"Hey, I'll take it." Carl shrugged. "Whatever gives me the right to call you 'Diz.' Although I have to say, your nickname's better than mine."

Max folded his arms, shoulders back. "Did he barge on over just to be annoying?"

Lizzie realized the one time Max acted like a bit of a jerk was in

145

reaction to Carl. She was getting a little tired of it. "Carl, did you find out anything about that kid, David Black?"

"You came to the right guy!" Carl stood proudly and produced a folded page from his jacket pocket. He unfolded it and handed it over. "Voila!"

Lizzie squinted in the dull early morning light. "I can barely read it – what's it say?"

"Well, there were a few David Blacks who kicked the bucket back in the 50's. None of them were teens, though. I did find out that there was a teenager named David Black who went missing back in the late 1940's, though. He just disappeared. The authorities must have decided he was a runaway, because I only found one article that advertised him missing. Did you notice the photograph? It wasn't a very good one. Really old and grainy, from the original newspaper ad."

Lizzie squinted harder, holding the page up closer to the street lamp. Max moved in, trying to get a closer look. The photograph showed an older kid with greased back hair and leather jacket. "This has to be him!" Lizzie stared. "What do you think, Max?" Max nodded in agreement.

"Max Fletcher?" Carl whispered, eyes wide. "He's here *right now?"*

"Yeah, Carl, he's been around me basically since the accident."

"Whoa." Carl's eyes nearly popped with excitement. "Is he coming to school with us?"

Max chuckled, amused by Carl's enthusiasm. He felt like a celebrity.

"He's followed me to school since Friday, too." Lizzie said.

Max huffed. "I'm not following you, Lizzie. I'm not a dog!"

"Okay, Max, okay!" Lizzie leaned closer to Carl's ear. "He's so sensitive!"

"I can hear you, Liz!" Max frowned.

The bus rolled up and Carl followed Liz to her seat so they could discuss David Black some more. Max didn't want to miss anything about Dave, so he sat in the seat behind them to listen in, beside a boy who was busy playing a game on his phone. Lizzie and Carl whispered their conversation, wanting to keep their investigation secret from other school bus riders.

"This kid, Dave, is a real jerk," Lizzie began to explain to Carl. "No disrespect intended to the dead. Seriously, though, he's pretty evil."

"So he's an evil spirit," Carl said. "I wonder if he's what other investigators call a 'shadow person.'"

"He wears dark clothes, but otherwise he just looks like a normal person to me," Lizzie explained. "Max says he can beckon demons from hell at his whim, so I'm not sure what his story is. It's almost like the opposite of what I've been learning to do. I'm learning how to use Holy Light to ward off these devils. So has Max. But this ghost, Dave, seems to have mastered the opposite task of bringing bad spirits – or demons – in to help him bully others."

"Wow," Carl sat back, overwhelmed. "Imagine that... a ghost bully. That's a pretty nasty thing to have at school."

Lizzie nodded. Carl had a good way of making the supernatural sound almost normal.

"So what do we do about it?" Carl sat up straight, looking at Lizzie.

She shrugged. "I have no idea."

Max butted in, his head between the two. "I've got one," he said. "But I'll need to hear every bit of info Carl has on Dave."

CHAPTER 26 - THE BATHROOM

As the bus approached the school that morning, Max was surprised not to be greeted by Dave's gang. Everything looked normal as they all exited the bus. Max was downright disappointed, having concocted a pretty decent plan. *No matter*, he shrugged. He was sure to come across Dave at some point in the day. After all, Dave did say he would "get him when he least expected it."

Half the day went by, and still no sign of Dave and his nasty cohorts. Max wandered the halls of the school, waiting for some kind of action. He had no interest in sitting in on any classes. Bored out of his mind, he walked by the trophy case, and stopped to look at the group photos of winning teams from decades past. There were group shots that went all the way back to the 1920's. Max leaned in, and found a shot with a plaque reading "Amherst Football Championship Team ~ 1948." He squinted at the faded black and white photo behind aged glass, scanning the faces, searching. Finally he stopped at one familiar face. It was Dave, all right.

"Wow, he was on the football team, too," Max muttered to himself.

Movement caught his attention from the hallway beside him. He noticed a girl walking down the hall. He recognized her. It was Mary, the girl who threw up on Friday after hearing about his death. She walked very slowly. Something didn't look right about her. She looked colorless, just like the black and white photographs on the trophy wall. He watched her closely, confused, starting to follow as she moped down the hallway. Something was wrong with her. He knew it.

He followed her until he saw her enter the girl's bathroom. Instinctively, he didn't want to follow any further, until he heard a gentle voice whisper behind him, "Go on, Max. She needs your help."

Still not used to moving through walls or doors, Max cringed with closed eyes and moved through the bathroom door. When he opened his eyes, he couldn't believe what he saw.

The bathroom was entirely covered with slippery black goo. The slime oozed over every surface, pulsating, as if it was alive. Max drew back with disgust. "What the heck is this?" He let the words escape from his lips. Mary was looking into the mirror blankly. It was the only surface not covered in black, slippery, sliding muck. Tears seeped from her eyes, but her face was stoic, her expression blank.

Max didn't know what to think, until he finally saw something familiar. A tall, cloaked shape moved out from one of the stalls, placing a clawed hand on Mary's shoulder. It turned to Max and smiled. Max shivered. It was the same being from Lizzie's room... the one who beckoned the spider-demons. It hissed a familiar phrase to him through lipless jaws. "She's mine!"

Max froze, and watched the scene reveal itself in slow motion. Mary set her purse up on the sink and withdrew a shiny object. At first Max thought it was a knife, but then realized it was a metal nail file. He watched as she began scratching the back of her hand with it. He ran forward, yelling, "Stop!"

The creature pushed him back and bared its teeth in a terrible grin. Max began to feel the slime from the floor begin to move up onto his feet. "Ack!" He shrieked instinctively. Realizing there was no Bertha, Bob or Lizzie to help him through this, it was time to find his strength and be the hero. He closed his eyes to concentrate, imagining the place of Light. The Light in his imagination grew brighter and brighter until it was bright as the sun. He held his arms out to reach for it, and then opened his eyes to see that not only was he holding the light, he was covered with it.

The creature sneered at him. "It will take more than that!" It hissed.

Max threw the ball of light at the creature and it screamed, stumbling backward. The slime where Max stood was sizzling and evaporating – turning to ash. The slime that first oozed from the walls even looked as though it was retreating through cracks – disappearing into nothingness to escape.

Mary collapsed on the floor and wept, dropping the nail file. Max knelt at her side. "I wish I could give you a hug," he said sadly.

Just as the tall creature took a step towards them, Lizzie miraculously entered the bathroom. At first she was shocked to see Max and prepared to scold him for being in the girls' bathroom. When she saw the scene in front of her, she gave Max a wide-eyed look that meant, *What did I miss?*

Max just looked at Lizzie in disbelief, ignoring the demon in the room. "I can't believe you just showed up like this! You have no idea. Mary really needs help. She was hurting herself!"

Lizzie's eyes widened, looking at the girl crying on the floor in front of Max. She knelt down with them. "Mary?"

Mary looked up at Lizzie, her face wet with tears. "Please don't tell anyone," she sobbed. "I don't know what I was trying to do. It just kind of happened. I was just trying to make the inside pain go away. I just feel dead inside." She fell into Lizzie arms and sobbed.

The monster grinned wide, looming over them. "You see? She's mine now!"

Lizzie wrapped her arms around the girl. She stroked her hair to calm her, the way her dad used to do. "Everything's gonna be okay," Lizzie whispered. She suddenly remembered a Peter Gabriel song her dad used to sing to her when she was down, and started singing softly, *"Don't give up..."*

Max saw as Lizzie stroked the girl's hair, Lizzie's whole body began to glow -- more than usual. But this time the glow was a pink color, and it seemed to bring color back to Mary.

"No!" The creature growled, and backed away.

Mary's skin slowly changed from gray to its natural hue. Max watched, mesmerized. "Keep doing that, Lizzie. It's helping her. It's amazing!"

Lizzie kept singing softly into Mary's ear until she felt Mary hug her back, squeezing her tight. "Thank you so much!" She wiped her face dry with her sleeve. "I can't tell you how badly I needed that."

Max looked around to see that the creature had disappeared.

Lizzie let Mary go, still sitting on the floor with her. "Are you going to be okay?" She asked.

Mary nodded. "I've just been feeling so hopeless these past few days. I don't know what's come over me. Everything just seems to be getting me down."

"Well, you let me know anytime you need a hug, okay, Mary?"

Mary smiled. "Okay."

As they stood up, Lizzie looked at the scratches on Mary's hand. "You really should have the nurse take a look at that," she said.

Mary nodded, wiping her eyes again. "Sure, okay. Thanks again,

Lizzie." She started out of the bathroom.

Lizzie blocked her. "I mean it, Mary, okay? If you start to feel sad like that again, you come and tell me. Nobody needs to suffer alone." She looked down. "I know how it feels."

Mary smiled and hugged her. "Thanks. You really helped me feel better." She let Lizzie go and smiled.

"Tell you what," Lizzie said, "You go straight to the nurse's office and I'll meet you there, okay? I just have to take care of something in here first, if you know what I mean." She chuckled.

"Okay, I'll see you there." Mary smiled and left the bathroom.

Max stared at Lizzie. "I can't believe you showed up when you did, Liz! That was like a miracle!"

Lizzie shrugged. "I just get these feelings sometimes. You know – like the voice of an angel on your shoulder telling you to do something? Well, this little angel was telling me I had to get to the bathroom, right away. Jeez, I'm glad I listened."

"Me too!" Max grinned.

"Well, I guess it's time for you to leave now, Max."

"Leave? What do you mean?" He was confused. "We're a team now, Liz. Do you just realize between the two of us, we might have just saved a girl's life! I don't know if I should leave... or if I want to leave. Maybe I'm supposed to stay here with you, Liz."

Lizzie blushed. "Oh, um... yeah. I'm glad to hear you say that, Max, but..."

"But what, Liz?"

"I actually meant for you to leave the bathroom, Max." She squirmed uncomfortably. "I have to pee."

CHAPTER 27
KILLING THE DARKNESS

Lizzie kept her promise to meet Mary in the nurse's office. Mary was lying down somewhere in the office when the nurse approached Lizzie, putting an arm around her. "I can't even begin to tell you what a blessing you are, young lady!" She said with soft eyes. "That girl is so lucky to have a friend like you."

Lizzie squirmed, not used to such compliments. "She's just a girl from my class, really. I don't know her all that well. I just saw she was sad and I wanted to help."

"Well, you're an angel in my eyes," the nurse smiled. "You did a wonderful thing, reaching out to a fellow student like that."

The nurse led Lizzie into a private room to ask some questions about what happened. There wasn't much that Lizzie could add to what the nurse already knew. It seemed that Mary decided to tell the nurse what happened, and her parents were contacted to pick her up to take her to the doctor for extra help. The school nurse kept thanking Lizzie and praising her, but Lizzie insisted she did what anyone else would have done.

Before leaving the nurse's office, she asked if she could say goodbye to Mary since her parents were coming to pick her up. Mary was lying on a cot in a private part of the office, where kids would normally lie when they had a fever at school. She turned her head and smiled at Lizzie when she entered the room. "Hi, Lizzie," she said, softly.

"Hi, Mary." Lizzie shyly walked over to her, hands behind her back. "I just wanted to say I'm really glad I was able to give you a hug when you needed it."

"Sometimes a hug makes all the difference." Mary smiled again, a little tear escaping the corner of her eye. She blinked, and she stared at the ceiling, looking deep in thought for a moment. "It was like..." She paused.

"Like... what?"

Mary looked at her again, another tear following the trail of the first one down the side of her face. "When you hugged me and started singing that little song, I felt like I was being brought back to life." She looked away. "I guess that sounds really weird, doesn't it?"

"No," Lizzie stepped closer. "It doesn't feel weird at all." She walked the rest of the way and sat on the edge of the cot. "To be honest, I've felt like that before too. Did you know my dad died?"

Mary propped herself up a bit with her elbows. "No, I'm sorry. I didn't know that."

"It was about a year ago, but it still feels like yesterday. I was starting to wonder if the pain I was feeling inside would ever go away."

"Is it starting to go away?"

"Well, to be honest I don't think I'll ever stop missing my dad... but I guess I'm not supposed to stop missing him anyway. Sometimes

I guess life just sucks. It's okay to be sad about things. What's important is not staying in that dark place. We just have to..." Lizzie stared, deep in thought. "We just have to find the light again -- even if it's just a small piece of light. The only thing that kills the darkness is the light."

Mary lay back down. "Wow, Lizzie, that's beautiful."

Lizzie snapped herself out of the trance, blushing. "I get a little too philosophical sometimes, I guess."

Mary smiled at her. "Even so... I'll have to write those words down when I get home and put it up in my room: *The only thing that kills the darkness is the light*. I love that."

Lizzie chuckled and stood. "Well, I guess my work here is done! Off to save another!"

The girls laughed.

As Lizzie opened the door to leave, she turned to wave. "Bye, Mary. I'll see you later, okay?"

"Yeah," Mary smiled, another little tear coming down. "I promise."

CHAPTER 28
WHAT DO YOU WANT ON YOUR TOMBSTONE?

While Lizzie disappeared in the nurse's office that afternoon, Max wandered around the school looking for signs of Dave and his gang. He almost felt unsettled by the fact they were nowhere to be found anywhere on the school grounds. Max decided to just wait in front of the building for school dismissal. It gave him quiet time to think without distractions. He hopped up on one of the empty cars parked in front, feet dangling off the side.

Tomorrow was the funeral. Apparently the light would return and he'd have his second chance to go into it. But if he did that, he would become like her dad, unable to ever communicate with Lizzie again. He couldn't believe how attached he was getting to this girl. She was definitely the best friend he'd ever had. Sure, she could be a real pain sometimes, but they were starting to feel like a team.

What would existence be like once he crossed into the light? Here in the In-Between there was danger, sure. But at least it wasn't boring. Who would he hang out with in the next dimension? Bob?

Thoughts raced through his head.

Finally he heard the dismissal bell, and there was a rumbling sound coming from inside the building of students rushing from their classrooms. He waited to catch Lizzie and Carl come out on their way to the bus.

"Carl... sheesh..." He muttered under his breath and shook his head. He had to admit he was kind of starting to like Carl. He had a knack for research, and was very eager to be helpful. *At least he doesn't seem quite interested in girls yet,* he found himself thinking. *And Liz doesn't seem interested in him either.* "Oh, *jeez!*" He winced and shook his head, scolding himself. "Am I crazy? Crushing on Dizzy Lizzie?" He let himself drop completely down with his back on the hood of the car, arms lying out at his sides. "And what's the point anyway? I'm freakin' dead! Yeah, brilliant move falling for someone when I can't even hold her hand! I'm such an idiot!"

"Hi, idiot!" Lizzie's voice startled him.

Max jumped off the car. "Oh, um, hi."

Lizzie had apparently just been walking by, and didn't bother stopping. Carl walked with her, blabbing about a blog he wanted to start. Lizzie turned to look at Max with a laughing smile and mouthed the words, *help me.* Max chuckled and followed.

On the bus, Carl and Lizzie sat together again, with Max in the seat behind them. They spent most of the trip discussing plans of how to get their parents to allow them to go to Max's funeral. The service was during school hours, so they knew they'd have to be very convincing that they truly wanted to go for the sake of Max, not as an excuse to skip school.

"I'm doubting my mom will get to take time off work to get us to the service," Lizzie said, "but she might at least let me go if I've got someone to take me there."

"My parents both work too," Carl said, thinking. "But I do have an idea. Just tell your mom you have a ride. I'll make sure it happens, trust me."

The bus stopped and they went their separate ways. Max followed alongside Lizzie down the path to her house along the graveyard.

They stopped as they noticed a tent way back in the cemetery, and a figure digging a new grave. "Wow." Max stared. "Is that my grave?"

Lizzie couldn't help but stare as well. "Jeez," she whispered, and looked at Max. "This must feel really strange to you."

Max couldn't even decipher what he was feeling, watching his own grave being dug. "Yeah, this is definitely super weird," he finally said.

Lizzie let out a single chuckle. "Super weird. That's true, Max." She nodded, and looked again at the men digging in the distance.

"Liz, I have to tell you something." Max decided he needed to explain.

"What?"

"Did you ever wonder why you can see me, but not your dad?"

Lizzie was curious about where this conversation was headed. "Actually, yes."

"Why don't you ever ask me about it, then?"

Lizzie shrugged, looking at the ground. "I don't know. I guess we've had so much else to talk about. I'm not sure how to bring it up. I guess deep down I'm afraid to know."

"Why would you be afraid? Afraid to know what?"

Lizzie shook her head. "I'm afraid that maybe he just doesn't want me to see him. Is that why?"

"No way, Liz!" Max turned to look straight at her. "That's not it at all."

"Well, why, then?"

"Well, I hope I can explain this right." Max thought hard. "Well, it's like the universe is designed like... like a big pizza."

Lizzie laughed. "A pizza?"

"Hey, don't laugh, okay? I'm trying my best, here. But yeah – You know how a pizza is built with layers of different toppings?"

"Sure."

"Okay, then imagine the dimension where all the living people exist only on the crust of the pizza, and most people – except you – are only aware of the crust."

"Okay. So I'm crusty."

"Stop making me laugh, Liz!"

Lizzie chuckled. "Sorry, Max, go on."

"So basically every layer of that pizza is a different dimension. You exist in the crust, I exist in the sauce, and your dad exists on the cheese dimension."

"Is there a pepperoni dimension?"

"Lizzie, please."

She chuckled again. "Sorry!"

"So, unlike anyone else living in the crust dimension, you have the special gift to see and talk to people like me who exist in the sauce. BUT, you can't seem to see or hear the ones like your dad who exist in the cheese dimension."

"Wow," Lizzie leaned against the nearest gravestone. "That actually makes sense." She stared at Max. "So wait a minute... Does that mean my dad has been with me all this time? I just couldn't see him?"

"That's right."

Lizzie looked as if she was in a trance. "So all this time... It wasn't because he didn't want to see me... It was because I couldn't see him."

Max nodded.

"Wow, thank you Max." She had tears in her eyes. "You have no idea what that means to me." Her face strained with a new thought. "But why? Why is my dad in some different dimension? What happened to put him in the cheese dimension, where I can't see or hear him? Why are you in the sauce and he's in the cheese?"

Max's face dropped. "Because I chose not to go into the light... and he did."

Lizzie looked up at Max, eyes widening. "Wait... so that means..." Her gaze shifted over to the man digging the grave.

Max finished for her. "It means when I go into the light tomorrow, we won't be able to hang out anymore. Well... I guess I can still visit you, but you'll never know I'm there." Max looked at his feet. "I guess you're probably getting tired of me anyway, though, right?"

"No." Lizzie didn't mean to let the word slip out like that, and decided to make a joke out of it. "Even though you are a royal pain in the butt."

Max smirked, and they both ended up gazing again at the gravedigger. The man seemed to be done with his job and was covering the empty grave, wiping his dirty hands on his jeans.

"I don't know what to do," Max said. "Here I'm getting my second chance to go into the light, and I don't know if I'm going to take it." He looked at Lizzie. "Is that stupid?"

Lizzie smiled at him, wiping a tear from her face. "Not stupid at all, Max." She stood up straight, and started walking to the house again. "Come on, let's enjoy this last night. We have tons of movies to choose from inside. After my homework, let's watch one, okay?"

Max followed alongside her, with a wry smile. "So we're going to the movies together, Liz?"

She laughed, holding up a hand. "Hey, don't get any ideas, now!"

Max smiled as they walked down the path.

Behind one of the gravestones, a dark figure watched. As they disappeared into Lizzie's home, the figure stood out from the shadows to reveal his greased back hairstyle. Although transparent, his leather jacket glistened in the moonlight.

David Black grinned. "I told you, Max Fletcher. I'll get you back when you least expect it."

CHAPTER 29 - THE GREAT ESCAPE

Today was Max's funeral. Lizzie and Max didn't talk much that morning, but their minds raced with scattered thoughts. Lizzie knew this could quite possibly be their last time to talk, but she found herself so caught up with thoughts, she couldn't say anything at all. As the clock ticked away in the classroom that morning, she breezed in and out of awareness, caught between her thoughts about Max and listening to the teacher spout the lesson for the day.

Finally it was time to excuse herself, and she headed to the office where Carl waited unknowingly with Max. Carl was dressed in a black suit, looking as if he was on his way to a business meeting. All that was missing was a briefcase.

"What's with the getup?" Lizzie looked him over.

"We're going to a funeral. This is the way you're supposed to dress, isn't it?"

"Oh." Lizzie suddenly felt a little self-conscious, checking her own outfit: jeans, sneakers and a plaid shirt overtop a purple T-shirt. She didn't think at all about how she should dress. She was too distracted by other thoughts.

"Don't worry," Carl said. "No one will notice."

Trying to brush it off, Lizzie switched her focus. "So, who's picking us up, then? Your mom or your dad?"

"Oh! There's our ride, right there!" Carl led them outside and waved down a red convertible that came screeching to a halt at the curb. Even with the windows up, they could feel the vibration of the Rap music.

The passenger window opened, and the music nearly blasted their eardrums. Carl ran over to the car, yelling for the driver to turn the music down, and then opened the door to get in the back seat. He waved to Lizzie. "Come, on! You can sit in the back with me, Liz!"

Lizzie cautiously approached, leaning in to get a peek at the driver.

Max followed. "Who the heck is that?" he asked.

Lizzie groaned. "You can sit in the front, Max, okay? I'm happy to sit in the back with Carl, trust me."

They entered the car while Carl was putting his seatbelt on in the back. He leaned over to Lizzie and said, "Trust me. You'll want to buckle up."

"I'll bet." She commented.

Max felt very strange getting into the front passenger seat. The last time he was in this position, of course, he died. Instinctively, he reached for the seatbelt, and was surprised to see that it actually moved when he grabbed for it. He stopped, looking at the driver to see if he noticed.

Sitting this close to the driver, he finally realized who it was – Dirk, the star football player at Steele High School. Max remembered seeing him on the field practicing football with the team.

Dirk turned around and flashed a smile at Lizzie. "Hop on up front if you want!" He yelled over the rap music.

"I'm fine back here," she nodded, leaning back in her seat. She leaned to talk in Carl's ear. "Doesn't he have classes to go to? Why is *he* taking us?"

"He'll do anything to get out of class," Carl said. "Besides, my parents couldn't help." He leaned forward in his seat and yelled, "You know where to go, right, Dirk?"

"I'm dropping you off at the Funeral home," Dirk answered. I got places to go though, midget, so I'll see you later."

"What?!" Carl yelled over the music while Dirk stepped on the gas, launching them away from the school, to the main road. "Wait – no! That's not how a funeral service works! First there's a service at the funeral parlor, and then we follow the hearse to the burial site. You're supposed to stay there with us for the service, and take us to the graveyard after, Dirk!"

Lizzie found herself squashed against Carl as Dirk whipped around the corner onto the main road. He hollered back to his brother in the seat behind him. "There is no freakin' way I'm staying for a funeral service, watching people cry over some dead kid!" Max leered at him. "The funeral home's walking distance to the graveyard, so just walk there after the service! It's not that far from home, so you don't need me to pick you up. I'll see you at home later, and remember our deal – no squealing to Mom and Dad!"

"Well, where the heck are you going, Dirk?" Carl asked. "You got a date with some airhead who's also skipping school today?"

"None of your business!" Dirk frowned, and turned the car into the driveway of the funeral home, stopping the car so quickly they almost got whiplash. "All right, get out!"

"Thank God," Lizzie muttered as she practically leaped from the vehicle. As she opened the door, she winced at the blast of inappropriate rap lyrics. She noticed the aghast looks of a few mourners entering the building.

Carl hurried out of the car to slam the door, muffling the noise.

Max stayed a moment in the front seat with Dirk. Reaching into the radio, he closed his eyes to focus and found the perfect music. Dirk jumped in his seat, as Dolly Parton's voice bellowed a classic country song over the speakers. "What the -- !!" He muttered, messing desperately with buttons and dials, trying to get back to his favorite station. "What's wrong with this thing?!"

Max exited the car, grinning at Lizzie from ear to ear. "That'll teach him!" He said, proudly.

CHAPTER 30 - THE VIEWING

"This is totally weird," Max muttered to himself as they entered the visitation room. It was filled with rows of chairs, with the casket housing Max's body at the very back of the room. Family members and friends that he hadn't seen in years were scattered about, talking softly and wiping tears from their eyes.

"You're telling me," Lizzie whispered. "This is totally weird for me too. Your body's over there in the casket, but here you are standing right beside me! This is the strangest thing I've ever experienced."

Carl overheard, and whispered, leaning in. "Oh my gosh, Max is talking to you right now?"

"Yeah, Carl, he's been with us the whole trip over here."

Carl slapped his forehead. "Oh, no. Can you tell him I'm so sorry about what my stupid brother said in the car? That was so insensitive!"

Lizzie smiled. "You don't need me to tell him, Carl. I'm not an interpreter. He can hear you just fine. Besides..." She crossed her arms. "I think Max got him back for it anyway."

"You mean... the radio? Dolly Parton – That was Max?" Carl laughed, and quickly slapped a hand over his mouth, reminding himself he was in a place of mourning. He took his hand away and whispered with a wide grin, "That was *so* awesome!"

The three wandered to the back of the room with their own set of emotions, heading for the open casket. The room was fragrant, flooded with floral bouquets and wreaths.

The three approached the coffin together, looking down at Max's body. He was dressed in the suit he wore to his aunt's wedding last year. He hated wearing suits and felt a little ticked off that they ended up burying him in one. "Why do they always have to bury people in fancy clothes and monkey suits?" Max frowned. "I mean, it's not like I ever really liked dressing that way when I was alive!"

Lizzie was caught with so many emotions, a tear came to her eye and she wiped it away quickly before Max could see.

Carl stared at Max's dead body, and leaned over to Lizzie. "Um, shouldn't we say a prayer or something?"

"Sure," she said, and motioned for him to start.

Carl bowed his head and folded is hands, Lizzie doing the same, feeling a little weird when the soul they were praying for was standing right beside her. "Dear God," he started, "Please welcome Max's soul into your Kingdom. I wish I would have gotten a chance to know him when he was alive, but thank you, God, for giving us the opportunity to get to know him a little better these last few days." Carl looked at Lizzie. "You want to add anything?"

Lizzie smiled at him. "Wow, Carl, that was a good prayer – I don't think I can top it." She bowed her head again, eyes closed, and simply said, "Amen."

Carl made the sign of the cross and they stood to turn and find a seat. Lizzie noticed that Max didn't follow. He just stood and stared down at himself. "God," he said softly, "Is it too late for me to pray?"

"It's never too late." He heard a familiar voice behind him. Turning around, he saw it was Bertha, dressed in a large polka dot black dress with obnoxiously puffy sleeves. Tucked in her hair was a little black net covering half her face, topped with an enormous, red carnation. She placed a gentle hand on his shoulder. "Trust me, Maxie. It's never too late to pray."

"I've never felt this scared before," Max said. "I feel so confused. I thought the light would be here today, but I don't see it anywhere yet. Am I too late? A part of me isn't even sure if I want to cross over into the light. At least I have Lizzie, here. And I'm even getting used to Carl. What's waiting for me in the light, anyway?"

"Those moments when you're confused... That's the best time to talk to God, Maxie. Why don't you give it a try?"

"I've never really tried before. Kinda feels like I'm sucking up."

"Go for it, trust me."

"How do I even talk to God, anyway? 'Now I lay me down to sleep, I pray the Lord my soul to keep?' I don't know any other prayers."

Bertha laughed. "Just be yourself, Maxie. Talk to Him just the way you talk to me. He'll love that. He loves everything about you."

"Yeah, right. That's why he let a car crash into me."

"Tragedy and suffering is just a part of living, Maxie. It's all part of being human. Some angels would gladly risk immortality for a taste of what you humans experience. They don't know what emotions feel like. They don't know what loss feels like. So they also don't understand the simplest joys you humans get to experience, like friendship. Without the darkness, it's hard to appreciate the light."

"So why are we bothering to fight the darkness, then, if it's such a normal part of life?"

"Because, Maxie, in case you haven't noticed, humanity is losing strength of character. They've become all too easy targets, losing hope and faith, and in some places almost worshipping the darkness. They need our help more than ever before. So up in the third highest dimension, we've been sending armies back down to earth who have earned their wisdom – gifted with special abilities."

"Like Lizzie?" Max's eyes widened.

Bertha smiled. "Yes, like Lizzie. There are millions of these Lightworkers living on earth, and they have been attacked most of all, to fear their gifts. Some have been driven by these demons to take their own lives – the worst outcome of all. They're such sensitive souls. Some just aren't strong enough to endure the pain of human existence. They need our help most of all."

"How do you know so much about all this, anyway, Bertha?"

Bertha winked. "I told you, honey. I'm not at liberty to reveal my sources. Let's just say I'm pretty close to the Man Upstairs. I'll leave you your privacy, sweetie. You go on and chat with Big Daddy up there."

She left his side and he was once again looking at himself in the coffin. He thought looking down at his own body would feel like meeting your twin self or something. But of course it wasn't like that at all. His body was empty. It was a thing, not a person... an empty shell. It didn't even look like him, he thought. It was obvious right then and there. He was no longer a part of that world. His body was dead, and he was starting a new life – a new existence – a new experience.

Max closed his eyes. "God?" He felt very awkward. "I assume you're listening to me somewhere. I've been so scared and confused, wondering what the right thing is to do. Everyone seems to be telling me to go into the light, but something's stopping me."

Max remembered his conversation last week with Bertha.

"Bertha spoke to me about finding my purpose. Well, actually, I remember she said the purpose would find me. And this might sound crazy, but…" He glanced over his shoulder to make sure Lizzie couldn't hear him. She was sitting a few rows back, talking with Carl. "I think I might know what that purpose is. Bertha told me that the more good decisions I make, the clearer the path would be. Well, going into the light just isn't feeling like part of that path. Not yet, any way. But I do know I am supposed to eventually cross over into the light. I just don't think today is the day." He opened his eyes again, hopeful. "Can you please give me a sign? I just need one simple sign today to show me what the right path is. I want to do the right thing." He wasn't sure how to end a prayer, so he simply ended with, "Thanks, God."

Suddenly he heard the voice of the Pastor who had come to speak for the funeral service. He called everyone to be seated, and the crowd gathered quickly into the seats. There were so many people, many had to stand in back. Max was surprised to see some of his old teachers. There were people he hadn't seen in years. Max sat on the step at the base of the casket, deciding to watch who had shown up. Mary was there too, accompanied by her parents. They took turns wrapping an arm around her shoulder for support and comfort.

Max noticed Bertha had vanished from the room, and he wondered if she was still around somewhere.

Finally he saw his dad enter the room, heading for the front reserved seats, followed by his mother who still wore the neck brace… and then he saw Perry. His mother pushed little Perry in a wheelchair. There was still an IV hooked up to her for fluids, but she looked better than she did at the hospital. Although she was obviously still hurting, she was dressed in her favorite party dress that she had also worn at their aunt's wedding.

Perry pointed excitedly to the casket, shouting with surprising energy, "Look, Mommy! SupaMax! SupaMax here!"

Max saw their parents try to suppress their tears from their daughter, trying to smile, saying, "Yes, sweetie. I know. That's Max up there. But he's resting now. You can't hug him, okay?"

"No, Mommy! I wanna go see Max! Max up there!" She kept pointing.

Mrs. Fletcher worried that she would try to wriggle free from the wheelchair, knocking out the IV. "Sweetie, you can see him in a little bit, okay? First we need to sit for a little while."

While Max's mom tried to calm Perry down, the Pastor began the service, welcoming everyone. He opened his bible, and began to read scripture. "God is our refuge and strength, an ever-present help in trouble. Therefore we will not fear..." He grabbed his throat as if he was about to cough, and then proceeded. "... will not fear, though the earth give way, and the mountains fall into the heart of the sea, though its waters roar..." He let out a loud cough. Max switched his gaze from the crowd, a little disappointed that they chose someone to run the service who apparently had a cold or something. "... There is a river whose streams make glad the city of God, the holy place *(Cough! Cough!)* where the Most High..." The Pastor begged everyone's forgiveness and to excuse him for a moment as a coughing fit overcame him. When he turned to leave the room, that's when Max saw what had attached itself to the Pastor's back.

Was there no end to the variety of creepy monsters in the afterworld? Max wondered. This creature looked like the skeleton of a monkey. Gray, leathery skin stretched over its bones, exposing every skeletal detail. A pair of horns topped its head for the final demonic touch. It was clawing its way through the back of the man's jacket. Max leapt to his feet, pointing at the man, trying to find the words, but realizing he was the only one in the room that could see what was happening.

Lizzie noticed Max's look of desperation, and glanced at the man, of course seeing nothing.

"How is this even possible?" Max said out loud. "This is practically a place of worship. Why would a demon even want to come in here? And how?!"

Finally Max saw the figure leering at him from the back of the room. Greased hair slicked back, with the same old leather jacket. He stepped forward boldly, straight down the center aisle, grinning the whole way. When he reached Perry's wheelchair, which stuck out into the aisle, he stopped. Dave's grin widened to its fullest point. "I'm gonna show you what misery really looks like," he said.

Max bolted from his spot. "Stop! No! Don't you dare touch her!" Dave opened his jaws wider than ever, and drew in a deep breath over Perry. Max could see her energy sucked out, and witnessed his little sister slump in her chair, weakening.

"Sweetie," his mother touched Perry's arm. "Are you okay?"

Perry didn't answer.

Lizzie watched in horror from her seat. What do I do? She thought. She felt totally trapped, surrounded by a group of people. Carl noticed. "What's going on?" He whispered.

"Ghost bully!" Lizzie whispered back. "Bad one!"

She couldn't stand it. Lizzie rose to her feet, shuffling through the seats, making it down the aisle and crouched down next to Perry, holding her little hand. "Hang in there, Perry! Be strong! I'll help you, okay?" Lizzie closed her eyes to concentrate and a glow of light began to form around her.

"Not this time!" Dave shouted in her ear. "You are a waste! You hear me? You are Nothing!"

Max saw Lizzie's light begin to fade, allowing Dave's words to seep in. "No! Don't listen to him, Liz! Please! I need you to help my sister!"

Using a powerful blast of energy, Dave punched Max so hard, he flew across the room. The energy was so strong, Max fell on one of the flower wreaths, knocking it over. A series of surprised mutterings filled the room.

Dave took a single step toward Max who lay dazed among the floral arrangements. "That's right! Take that, Fletcher! I'm the boss around here, and don't you forget it!" He raised his arms, closed his eyes, and lifted his chin high. Max watched as the room filled with darkness, and creatures began to crawl from every shadow.

Max's fears were replaced with rage. He rose, staring down his opponent. "Stop screwing with my funeral, you turd wad! Stop messing with my sister! And leave Liz alone!"

"Or what? You'll kill me?" Dave laughed.

Max marched closer. He closed his eyes, trying to calm himself. Time to activate his plan. "Yes, Dave. I'm going to kill you."

Dave laughed even louder. "You can't be serious!"

Max sidled right up to Dave until their faces almost touched. "Oh, yes, Dave. Very serious." Max reached up and grabbed Dave by the head, clasping with both hands covering Dave's ears.

Dave struggled. "What are you doing?"

Max concentrated, closing his eyes. He remembered the technique he used for the radio to access the different channels, finding Dolly Parton instead of the rap music to taunt Dirk. This time he needed to access something else. He focused, reaching inside Dave's memories, for the moment he was searching for. He tried his best to tune out the creatures snarling around him, trying to get to his sister, Perry. Lizzie kept holding her, trying to keep her own light alive to protect her.

"I found it!" Max blurted out.

"Found what? Let me go!" Dave continued to struggle.

"In 1944 you disappeared from your home, Dave. You ran away, didn't you?"

Confused, Dave began to panic. "Let go of me!"

Max felt lost in Dave's memory, watching it as if it was a movie. He saw Dave's memory of sneaking out of his parents' house to skip town with a girl he had fallen for at school. "You and your girlfriend ran away together." Max muttered, in a total trance. "You wanted to get married, but you were both too young."

Dave had enough. "Get out of my head! Shut up!"

"You were the one with the idea. You talked her into it."

"Shut up! Shut up!"

"You brought a bottle of your dad's liquor with you, and you both drank it up to celebrate while driving out of town."

"Get off me! Stop!"

"You made it as far as New York State, and that's when you missed the turn, driving you both off the bridge."

Dave's eyes were desperate. "No! No!" His voice started breaking down. "Please! Please stop!"

Max opened his eyes. "Your parents searched everywhere for you, Dave. Our friend, Carl, looked it up. They died several years ago, but they never stopped hoping you were out there. They never gave up hoping their son would come back to them."

Dave began to weep in Max's arms, broken. "Please stop. Please... I beg you." He slumped down to the floor, Max keeping his arms wrapped around him.

"It's okay, Dave. It was an accident."

"It's not okay," Dave shook his head, continuing to sob. "If I hadn't been drinking... If I hadn't talked her into leaving with me... She'd still be alive... We'd still be alive... and..."

"And what, Dave?" Max leaned in.

"She was pregnant." Dave wailed. "I lost everything! All it took was one lousy mistake... and I lost everything that was ever important to me!" He broke down completely and allowed himself to lie in Max's arms.

Max suddenly felt a presence behind him, and the creatures snarling in the room seemed disturbed by this new entity. Max turned around and saw a familiar face. "Bob! It's about time you showed up!"

That wasn't the only thing that had suddenly appeared. A bright light shone down on the casket, like a tunnel waiting for a passenger. Max was stunned. The walls of light moved like a rippling stream.

Bob kneeled down to meet them on the floor. "I have a message for your friend Dave, here."

Dave looked up at Bob. "Who are you?"

"Who I am isn't important, Dave. What really matters is whom I know. I know your mom, your dad, your girlfriend, and your baby. They've been waiting for you a long time, kid."

Dave looked up with an expression that surprised Max. He looked like a different person. Instead of a face filled with anger and resentment, he wore an expression of love. "Are you serious?" Dave whispered.

Bob turned, pointing to the light. "See for yourself," he said.

Max squinted and saw the figure of a young lady. She wore a snug white sweater and a checkered skirt. She held a tiny baby in her arms. "Please come home, Dave," she said.

Dave's eyes were wide.

Max noticed the entire room was brighter. The darkness was gone and the creatures must have scurried away. Lizzie remained at Perry's side, holding the little girl's hand, but now it seemed more for her own strength. She couldn't believe the transformation she was witnessing. All she could see was Max, Dave, and the light – but she knew much more was going on. She couldn't wait to hear all about it the next time she talked with Max. Or was Max going into the light now? *Please, Max,* she thought to herself. *Please don't go yet.*

Dave rose from the floor and Max finally let go of him. Dave walked trance-like toward the light over the casket. "I've missed you more than you can ever know," he told the young woman in the light. Before leaving, he turned to Max and Lizzie one more time. "I can't thank you guys enough. I've been a jerk for so long... He nodded at Max... But that Dave is dead now!" He smiled.

"Told ya," Max smiled back.

Dave nodded again and turned back to the light. His feet left the floor as the tunnel sucked him up through the ceiling.

"Well, that's not something you see every day, is it?" Bob put a hand on Max's shoulder. "Guess you're next, right kid?"

Max looked over at Lizzie who looked a little sad. She watched Dave go into the light and was quite amazed by the whole thing, but knew this was Max's opportunity as well.

"I don't have to leave quite yet, do I?" Max asked Bob. "I mean, I'd like to be there for the burial part of things. The light will still be there for that part, right?"

"Sure," Bob said, "but I wouldn't dilly dally too long this time. It might be your last shot."

CHAPTER 31 - FINAL RESTING PLACE

Lizzie and Carl made their way down the street, chatting about what happened while Bob and Max waited for them at the burial site. Flowers had been set up at the grave already, under the tent. Max looked up and saw the tunnel of light leading way up into the open sky. Max remembered looking at photos of waterspouts. It looked a lot like that, but much less intimidating. Now that they were in a quiet place, Max could actually hear a sound coming from the light. It was like the sound of wind mixed with the faint, echo of music – but no music he'd ever heard before. He couldn't tell if it was instrumental or vocal.

Bob walked up beside him. "You're having second thoughts, aren't you?"

Max wasn't prepared for this discussion. "Yeah. I know it sounds stupid, but..."

"I understand, trust me. This place is tempting. Everything you know is here – everyone you care about. It's hard to leave that behind."

"It's not just that, though," Max shook his head. "I feel like I might have a purpose here."

"What purpose?"

"Bertha told me everyone has a purpose. Liz is finally starting to understand what hers is, and that's great. But I think I know what mine might be, too." Max put his hands on his hips. "I think I need to stay here, Bob. Carl, Liz and I... We make a pretty good team, don't you think?"

Bob grinned, raising an eyebrow. "You're an odd team, that's for sure."

Max smiled, crossing his arms and looking up at the vortex of light in the sky. "Do you know if I'll ever get another chance? You know... to cross over?"

Bob gazed at the swirling light above. "I'm not sure, kid. There are still things I'm trying to understand, myself. Bertha would know more than me on that subject."

"Say, who is Bertha, anyway?" Max turned to face Bob. "She said she didn't want to show me who she really is. I don't get it. Why the big secret?"

Bob smiled. "Trust me, kid... and trust her, too. Once you find out who she really is, the relationship changes. Right now you see her as a friendly wise woman dropping in occasionally to help you out in a pinch or to give guidance. That's how she wants you to see her, and that's the way it's going to stay."

Max shrugged, giving up. "Whatever, okay. I still don't understand what the big deal is."

People started to gather. His father wheeled Perry under the tent. His mother repositioned the seats to make room for the wheelchair. The Pastor rushed over to help. More people showed up to the gravesite than expected. There were enough seats for immediate family, but most people ended up standing. Lizzie and Carl tried pushing through the crowd to get as close as possible. Lizzie pointed up at the vortex, whispering to Carl what she was seeing. His eyes were wide as he heard the description, amazed.

Lizzie then scanned the crowd, looking for Max. He saw her look of desperation, and when their eyes locked, she waved at him to follow her. Telling Carl she'd be right back, she pushed out of the crowd and walked to an empty area, to speak privately with Max.

"Oh my gosh," she shook her head, not knowing what to say to him. Tears filled her eyes. "I can't believe what happened back there at the funeral home! Can you believe it?"

"It was pretty neat, yeah." Max said.

Lizzie laughed. "Neat? Max, you were incredible! I don't know how you did what you did – but you saved that boy, and you saved the rest of us in that room!"

"And you saved my sister, Liz." Max smiled. "Thanks for protecting her! If you hadn't done that, I wouldn't have been able to concentrate enough to do any of that."

"We make a pretty good team, Max." She smiled, another tear coming.

"That's what I was just telling your dad." Max grinned.

"My dad?" Lizzie's eyes widened. "My dad's here? Where is he right now?"

"I'm over here, kiddo," she heard a voice say. It was coming from the vortex, which touched the ground a few yards from the tent, away from the crowd.

"Daddy!" Lizzie practically flew to him, feet barely touching the ground as she ran, almost running through him. She stopped inches away. "Daddy," she whispered. "I've missed you so much."

Bob smiled tenderly. "Same here, kiddo." He reached out his

arms. Lizzie didn't know if she'd be able to hug her father, but she didn't care. She stepped into the vortex and reached her arms around her father. She felt his arms wrap around her, feeling the warmth of his energy. "I love you so much. -- You and your mom."

"I wish I could tell her 'Dad says hi,' but I guess that'd be a bad idea." Lizzie smiled, tears seeping from her eyes.

"She's starting to catch on to your secret anyway, Lizzie," he warned. "You might have to let her in on it. She's starting to really worry about you. She's confused."

Lizzie looked up at her father's face. "So you've been looking in on us. Every day?"

"Every day," he grinned.

Lizzie hugged him tighter. "I don't ever want to let you go! I wish I could hold you forever, Dad."

"But you do need to let me go," he said softly. "And now that you have Max to help look after you, I guess I can start letting go a bit too. That boy really cares about you."

"I love you more than anything, Dad!"

"Ditto, kiddo," he smiled.

She laughed and squeezed him tighter. "Please don't leave again, Daddy."

"I never left you in the first place, Lizzie." He held her shoulders firmly and pushed to look her straight in the eyes. "All you need to do is call me, kiddo, and I'll be there for you. I need to give you space, though, so you can start depending on yourself for a change. You are so strong. You can handle things on your own now." He looked at Max and Carl who were watching from the gravesite. "You have your friends now. They will help give you the extra strength you need."

"But Max is leaving!" Lizzie cried.

Bob raised an eyebrow. "Is he?"

Lizzie looked over her shoulder at Max and Carl, and gave her father one last hug. "Daddy, I love you so much."

"And I'm so proud of you, kiddo," he said, hugging her back. "Now, go see your friends, okay? I'll be around when you need me."

Lizzie let her father go and stepped out from the vortex. She waved to her dad as he disappeared, dissolving into the light. "Bye, Daddy," she whispered.

Max rushed over. "Lizzie, are you okay?"

"I don't know," her chin quivered. "I feel like once you leave, Max, I'll be alone again."

"What about Carl?" Max asked.

"Carl's getting to be a great friend, yeah," she looked over at Carl who was trying to wave her over to the service at the gravesite. "But, well, you know..."

"Know what?"

Lizzie wiped her eyes, getting frustrated. "Seriously, Max, do I have to spell it out for you?" She sighed. "It's just that... you're like... my best friend."

Max beamed. "Same here, Liz."

"So when are you leaving, then? To cross over into the light?" Lizzie crossed her arms.

"I'm not going," Max smiled and shook his head.

"What?"

"I'm not going, Liz."

"What do you mean? I thought you had to go?"

"It's a choice, Liz, like everything else. I have to follow my own path. Like you!" He motioned to Lizzie. "You finally discovered your purpose! You're a Lightworker! And you're awesome at it, Liz!"

Lizzie blushed.

"And I think now I know what my purpose is." He glanced over at the vortex. "And it doesn't involve going into the light... at least not yet. My place is right here, in the In-Between... with you, Liz."

Lizzie felt an electric charge run through her body when she heard those words, and it made her blush again. She looked down at her shoes. "So you're not leaving me?"

Max took a step closer, and put every bit of energy he had into his fingers as he touched her hand. "I'm not going anywhere."

She felt the warmth of his energy touch her hand, and she spread out her fingers, letting it surge through her palm. She opened her mouth, about to say what was in her heart –

"Hey, Diz!" Carl nearly bumped into her, running from the gravesite. "What the heck is going on over here? You, like, missed the whole burial service! They're placing roses on the casket now. Here!" Carl handed her a red rose, panting from his run. "I saved one for you! I thought we could go put them on the casket together!"

Lizzie shook her head, taking the rose from Carl's hand. "Yeah, let's do that, Carl." She smiled, looking at Max who laughed. "Max is joining us, by the way."

"You mean he isn't going into the light yet?" Carl asked.

"No, Carl." Lizzie and Max exchanged a glance. "He's staying."

"Cool!" Carl grabbed her hand, pulling her over to the coffin. He placed his rose on the pile that was already there, and made the sign of the cross.

Lizzie was about to place her rose on the casket. She stopped, placing her hand on it, instead. She pressed the rose to her chest. "I'm glad I got to know you, Max Fletcher," she smiled, and walked away, keeping the flower as a memento.

CHAPTER 32 - "I SEE YOU."

Max watched his parents shake hands with the last people to leave the gravesite. A caregiver stayed with Perry while they spoke with some family members who wanted to help transporting personal items – photographs, albums – left back at the funeral parlor.

Max stepped over to his little sister. She had fallen asleep and was dozing peacefully with the nurse at her side. "I'm glad you survived, little bud," he said.

He saw her squirm a bit in her sleep.

"I'll keep an eye on you, okay? As often as I can. I'll be busy with my new friends. We have a lot of good work to do." He chuckled. "I guess I kind of ended up as a bit of a superhero, after all, Perry. SuperMax to the rescue!" He laughed, and looked down. "I wish you could see me now. You'd probably tell me to wear a cape. Ha! Yep, SuperMax, that's me! You'd be surprised. I have some pretty cool super powers, too."

Max looked back up, chuckling, and his face dropped immediately, frozen with shock. Perry woke up, and her eyes were wide open... staring directly at him.

Max stared back at her, stunned. *"Perry..."* He whispered. *"... Do you see me?"*

His eyes widened as he heard her giggle, and point to him. "See you, Max! See you!"

The nurse sitting beside Perry stared at the toddler, confused.

Max didn't know what to do. Perry was too young to understand the delicacy of the situation. He looked around to see if his parents noticed.

Perry kept chatting away. "I see SupaMax! I see SupaMax!"

The nurse tried to shush her, concerned.

Perry paused, cocking her head like a confused puppy. She pointed, looking at something farther away. "Who that?"

Max looked around, wondering what she was talking about. His eyes stopped at a figure in the distance. It was someone he'd never seen before, but it was definitely another dead person. He was an older teen, looking to be about the same age as Dirk, but not nearly as athletic-looking. Max raised a hand to wave hello, which startled the boy. He straightened up sharply and bolted.

"Hey, wait!" Max called out, but the boy was already gone.

"He says he's sorry," Perry said.

Max turned and squatted down next to her again. "What? Who?"

"That boy. He told me when I was asleep. I was asleep a lot in the hospital, and he told me a lot of things."

Max leaned close. "What did he tell you, Perry?"

"He says he's really sorry. He didn't mean to hit us. He said he forgot to take his pills."

Max's eyes were wide, and he stood up again, looking for the boy. "Oh my God. Where the heck did he go? Who is he?"

Perry shrugged. "I dunno. He's really nice, though."

"*Nice?!*" Max fumed. "He's *nice? He killed* me, Perry! He put *you* in the hospital!"

"I'm okay." Perry squinted, confused. "And you're not killed, Max." She smiled wide. "You SupaMax!"

The nurse was progressively growing more concerned and suspicious the longer Perry babbled. Max decided he would wait until they were alone before explaining anything further to her.

Max looked for Lizzie and Carl, and saw they had retreated to the opposite side of the graveyard, perched on Lizzie's usual gravestone hangout spot by her house. "I'll see you later, Perry," Max smiled. "You keep getting better, okay? And take care of mom and dad for me!"

Perry smiled up at him, grinning wide. He walked away and waved, watching her wave back with her little arm as he joined Lizzie and Carl.

"We still have some time left before our parents get home," Carl said. "How about we walk over to the Hastee Tastee? I'm in the mood for ice cream."

"Sounds good to me," Lizzie said. "Wanna join us, Max?"

"Yeah, sure!" Max faked an excited tone. "I'll have a double scoop of mint chocolate chip in a waffle cone! Oh – Hey! Wait a minute, I forgot..." He laughed, scoffing. "... I'm *dead!*"

Lizzie laughed. "I'll order one and you can watch me eat it."

"As fun as that sounds," Max said sarcastically, "I think I'll pass. You two live people enjoy your ice cream."

"Come on, Max. Remember, we're a team now!" Lizzie smiled.

Carl grinned. "Yeah, we're the Amherst Paranormal Society!"

"I think we need a better name," Max said. "I don't know if 'society' applies to a pair of kids and a dead guy."

"We'll talk about it over ice cream, Max." Lizzie waved at him to join them as she and Carl hopped off the gravestone to head across the street.

CHAPTER 33 - SLEEP TIGHT

That night, Max told Lizzie he would help watch over her, as he had been doing almost every night since the accident.

As Lizzie wrote in her journal, Max paced the room, thinking about the boy in the graveyard.

"This might sound like a really stupid question, considering you were buried today." Lizzie said. "But are you okay?"

Max huffed. "Peachy."

Lizzie rolled her eyes, returning attention to her journal. "Okay, I'll just get back to my writing here. Hmm... Let's see..." She moved her pen across the page. *"Max is acting really weird tonight. Perhaps the ectoplasm is riding up his butt crack, creating severe irritation."*

"Don't write that! Hey!" Max stomped over.

Lizzie chuckled. "Then just tell me, Max. What's going on?"

Max started pacing again. "Well, for one thing, Perry can see me now."

Lizzie's eyes widened. "Whoa! What? How?"

"I don't know. Maybe it's because she died for one moment in the hospital. Maybe that did something. Or maybe she's like you, and was just born with it. I have no clue."

"So what's the other thing?" Lizzie prodded.

"Huh?"

"You said, 'for one thing.' So, what's the other thing?"

"Well, it's pretty heavy."

"Try me. In the past few days I've killed off a demon, protected a schoolmate and a toddler from spiritual warfare, and hugged my dead father. Whatever you want to talk about, I think I can handle it, Max."

"Okay." Max sat on the end of her bed. "In the graveyard I saw the guy who killed me."

"Whoa."

"Yeah. And I guess he talked to Perry somehow while she was unconscious in the hospital. She said he's sorry."

"Whoa."

"Yeah. I mean, I really don't know what to do. It was easier when I didn't know anything about the person in the other car. Now I find out that person is somewhere around here too. What the heck do I do about that? Do I confront him? Do I tell him off?"

"Max, he apologized to your sister."

"So what? *She's* not dead! *I* am! *I'm* the one that died! He should apologize to *me*, Liz! To *me!*"

Lizzie remembered what her therapist told her. It was one of the few things that stuck. "Max, go ahead and feel angry tonight. And then tomorrow, at the rise of the sun and a new day, let that anger go."

"Let it go? Seriously, Liz?"

"Just because you have the right to feel angry, it doesn't mean it's okay to stay angry, Max. Staying angry makes you sick."

"Ha! Sick? Hmm. I'm dead already, Liz. I can't get sick!"

"Are you completely stupid, Max? Don't you remember Mary at school, and what happened to her in the bathroom?"

Max paused. How could he forget? He couldn't get that oozing, pulsing blackness out of his memory. He wished he could forget.

"She was under attack, remember? She might have killed herself if we didn't help her. I've been thinking a lot about that day. Those demons are working to weaken us, Max. They want us to feel sadness and hatred. That's how they get people... even *dead* people, Max."

Max bowed his head, frowning. "So you're telling me to just get over it?"

"I'd never say that, Max. Look at me. My dad died. I was a wreck. I was still a wreck when you met me. Heck, I don't know if I'll *ever* get over it."

"So how do I let that anger go?"

Lizzie looked down at the journal in her lap. "I don't know, Max." She looked back up at him again, with a little smile. "But we'll figure it out, okay? The important thing is that you're not alone, Max." She smiled a little wider, and reached her hand out to him. "And neither am I anymore."

Max smiled back and reached for her hand. Before he could try to touch her fingers, there was a knock on the door. Max stood, startled.

"Lizzie! Done with your journal time?" Mother called through the door.

"Yeah, Mom!" Lizzie closed her journal for the night and laid it next to her lamp on the bed table, beside her neglected MP3 player and earplugs.

Her mother entered and sat on the side of her bed to say goodnight. "How was your day, sweetie?"

Well, Mom, let's see... I saw Dad today.

"You were able to get a ride from school to get to that boy's funeral this afternoon, right?"

"Yeah, thanks for the permission slip, mom."

"Of course." She stroked Lizzie's hair. "Are you doing okay?"

"I know it sounds strange, but yes. I'm actually doing great, Mom." Lizzie smiled.

Her mother was relieved. "I'm so glad." She kissed her daughter on her forehead. "Funerals really help to bring closure."

"On many levels." Lizzie grinned.

Her mom said a final goodnight and turned off the light, closing the door behind her.

"Goodnight Max," Lizzie whispered.

"Goodnight, Liz." Max smiled, leaning in his usual spot against the wall.

The moonlight shone through Lizzie's window. The curtains were open and the blinds up. Max stood and walked over, gazing at the quiet graveyard. A light mist covered the grounds. It looked like Halloween out there. The tent from the burial service was taken down, and the casket was lowered and covered with a fresh mound of earth.

Will I ever get used to this? He thought. This whole "being dead" thing still felt weird. But then, it hadn't even been a whole week since he died. He laughed at himself. *Well, at least I have eternity to get used to it.*

He glanced down and saw the skinny vase placed on Lizzie's desk, housing the red rose. He smiled, thinking how nice it was for her to keep it. He walked back to his spot against the wall and slid down on the floor to rest his energy.

A house spider crawled along the wall of Lizzie's room, and

stopped as it approached the darkest corner. The spider turned around, instinctively avoiding the dark energy lurking there. The tall, dark figure stood, camouflaged, waiting for the right moment to strike again.

ABOUT THE AUTHOR

Wendy Fedan is a freelance artist who recently moved to Amherst, Ohio with her husband, two kids, and psycho kitty. She also teaches classes to various age groups about writing and composing books, as well as creative workshops. Wendy loves speaking to kids and adults about creativity and writing and has visited public schools to share her own journey and help inspire young writers.

Contact Wendy through her website: http://wfedan.weebly.com/